HIGH SCHOOL MUSICAL

STORIES FROM EAST HIGH #1

BATTLE OF THE BANDS

By N.B. Grace

Based on the Disney Channel Original Movie
High School Musical, written by Peter Barsocchini

Parragon

Bath New York Singapore Hong Kong Cologne Delhi Melbourne

First published by Parragon in 2007
Parragon
Queen Street House
4 Queen Street
Bath BA1 1HE, UK

ISBN 978-1-4075-0342-4

Printed in China

CHAPTER ONE

The first bell had just rung at East High School when Chad Danforth spotted Troy Bolton across the courtyard.

"Hey, Troy!" Chad yelled, smiling broadly.

But Troy didn't hear him. He was standing with his friend Gabriella Montez. Their heads were bent towards each other as they talked. Troy said something that made Gabriella giggle. Then she said something that made him laugh. Chad rolled his eyes. That was sweet and all, but enough was enough . . .

"Hey!" Chad called again as he walked towards them, waving his hand in the air. "Troy! What's up?"

Finally, he caught Troy's eye. Gabriella smiled a quick hello at Chad and said, "I'll see you guys at the assembly." Then she waved goodbye. Troy looked after her as she headed inside the building.

"Hey, Troy! How you doin', man?" Chad greeted his friend with a complicated high five, low-five, round-the-back, over-the-top handshake.

Troy grinned. Saying hi to Chad was as athletic as driving to the hoop for a slam dunk, he thought. "Not bad," he said. "Pretty awesome, in fact."

"Awesome? What happened, did you get an early recruitment call from the NBA?" Chad joked.

"No, I'm just in a really good mood."

Chad raised his eyebrows. "Because . . ."

"Because of Gabriella," Troy said. "You know, I've been spending a lot of time with her."

"Oh, yeah." Chad rolled his eyes. "I know."

Troy got a distracted look on his face. "She's so sweet and smart and talented–"

"Yeah, yeah, yeah." Chad made a get-on-with-it gesture. "I know. We all know."

"What?" His friend looked at him, puzzled by his exasperated tone. "Is something wrong?"

"No. Well, yeah. I mean, not wrong exactly . . . the thing is, I've been meaning to say something . . . " Chad stopped, flustered.

"Chad, come on! Just tell me! What is it?" Troy tried to laugh, but he was getting worried.

"It's just . . . Gabriella's great and everything, but you're not hanging with your boys anymore. We kinda–" Chad looked nervously over his shoulder to see if anyone was standing close enough to hear him, "–we kinda miss you, dude."

"We see each other every day at practice!" Troy said, surprised.

"Yeah, but Troy, that's not hangin'. You gotta

put in some quality time, especially with me and Jason and Zeke." Chad looked at him earnestly. "The four of us are the core of the team, you know? We gotta stay tight."

"Sure," Troy said. "No problem. I mean, I like doing stuff with you guys, I really do."

Chad grinned, relieved. "Good. We'll set something up. Maybe this weekend? Just the guys."

"Sounds great." Troy smiled and tried not to look worried. He and Gabriella were planning to take a long bike ride on Saturday and maybe see a movie on Sunday . . . but hey, there were 48 hours in a weekend, right? He could make time for everybody! No problem!

"Come on, let's get to the assembly," he said to Chad. "I heard a rumour that Principal Matsui has a big announcement today . . . "

Troy and Chad quickly found Gabriella in the auditorium and sat next to her. A few rows behind them, Sharpay and Ryan Evans were sitting with a gaggle of kids from the drama club.

Everyone was chatting about what they did last weekend, what they planned to do next weekend and how endlessly long the time stretched between weekends.

Finally, Principal Matsui walked onto the stage and tapped the microphone. After a deafening burst of feedback, he called out, “Good morning, East High students! Welcome to another great week of learning and fun!” He paused for a moment, waiting for the students to applaud wildly, but – as usual – was met only with quiet murmurs and chuckling.

He sighed and hurried on. “First, a few announcements.” He ran down the usual list of SAT preparation classes, pep rallies and special assemblies. Then he said, “But I have saved the best for last! I’m very excited to announce that the school is going to stage a Battle of the Bands next month in order to raise money for our new tennis courts.”

A buzz of excitement filled the auditorium as everyone started whispering to each other.

Troy gave Chad a nudge. "Here's your big chance, buddy. All those years of playing air guitar in your bedroom are finally going to pay off."

"Look who's talking," Chad replied. "Remember when you spent a month practising air jumps off the couch?"

Gabriella grinned at Troy. "Air jumps? Really?"

"I've got a few moves," Troy said modestly.

"If I may have your attention, please," said Principal Matsui. When the room was quiet enough, he continued. "This is a thrilling opportunity for all you rock stars out there, so I hope we have a big turnout! All you have to do is get a bunch of your friends, form a group and sign up in the front office by this Friday!"

Sharpay turned to her brother, Ryan, and Alicia and Charlotte, her drama club friends. Well, not exactly *friends.* They were more like girls who were destined to always be understudies, which was, of course, why Sharpay liked them. "We should totally do this!" she said.

"Totally," Ryan agreed with enthusiasm.

Alicia and Charlotte giggled with delight at being chosen by Sharpay.

Principal Matsui finished by saying, "Ms Dermot will assign rehearsal space on a first-come, first-served basis. Now, it's time for everyone to get to class, but remember – I'm looking forward to hearing a rockin' good show from all of you!"

The students poured out of the auditorium, talking enthusiastically about the Battle of the Bands competition. Sharpay was lost in a day-dream, envisioning herself in her favourite spot in the world – onstage, in the spotlight, with all eyes fixed on her . . .

"We'll be awesome!" she said, a note of steely determination in her voice.

"Beyond awesome!" Ryan interjected. "Awe-some to the tenth power!"

His sister shot him a confused look. Some-times she had no idea what Ryan was talking about. "First of all," she said, firmly regain-ing control of the conversation, "what could be more perfect than me as the lead singer–"

"Absolutely," Ryan said.

"And you two–" she indicated Alicia and Charlotte, "–as backup singers–"

"Of course." The girls nodded obediently.

"–of an absolutely fabulous girl group!" Sharpay finished.

"Um . . . girl group?" Ryan echoed.

"Yes!" she cried. "It'll be so retro!"

"But, Sharpay, if it's a *girl* group . . ." Ryan stopped, puzzled, then tried again. "I mean, what about me?"

Sharpay ignored him. "We'll wear miniskirts and knee-high boots and have our hair done in that sixties style," she said, thinking out loud. "And of course, we need a really cool song–"

"Sharpay?" Ryan tried again. "When you say 'girl group', do you mean that it will actually have, um, only girls in it?"

"What?" His sister stared at him blankly. "Well, of course, Ryan! What a silly question!"

She turned back to her friends. As they began

chatting eagerly about song possibilities, Sharpay didn't notice Ryan's crestfallen look, his slumped shoulders, or the way his feet dragged as he walked slowly away.

"Now, we'll have to pick a song that really showcases the lead singer," she was saying. "Not to mention a song that offers the possibility of some showstopping choreography . . ."

Gabriella, Troy and Chad continued their conversation as they left the auditorium. "So what are your best rock-star moves?" Gabriella asked Troy, a teasing note in her voice.

He shrugged, grinning. "Oh, you know. The windmill–" he pantomimed swinging his arm around and strumming chords, "–the head bob–" he nodded his head in time to imaginary music, "–just stupid stuff like that."

"That's not all," Chad said to Gabriella. "He actually knows how to play guitar."

"Well . . . only three chords," Troy said. "But that's all you need to play 95 per cent of all rock songs ever written, so . . ." He stopped dead in his tracks and looked at Chad. "Hey! I just had a great idea!"

Chad raised his eyebrows.

"We could form a band!" Troy said eagerly. "I could teach you guys how to play guitar – well, three chords, anyway."

"Awesome!" Chad's eyes lit up at the idea of taking the stage in full rock-star mode.

Gabriella's eyes sparkled. "That's such a good idea–"

"And you know how you were saying that I needed to hang with the guys more?" Troy went on to Chad. "This is a perfect way to do that! We can hang out and jam together, just us guys!"

Gabriella's smile dimmed. "Oh. You're going to be in a band with your basketball friends."

"Yeah!" Troy turned to her, grinning with excitement. He didn't notice how flat her voice was, or the way she tried to smile but couldn't quite manage it, or the way she bit her lip with disappointment. "Man, this is going to be awesome!"

"You got that right!" Chad was grinning, too. "Now, the first thing we need is a cool name. That's key. An awesome name can *make* a band. How about The Three-Pointers?"

"The Three-Pointers?" Troy repeated dubiously. "Um, I don't know . . . doesn't that make it sound like there are only three of us? And we're a pack of hunting dogs?"

"C'mon, man, it's perfect! No? Okay, how about B-Ball Boyz?"

As they turned the corner, still debating band names, Gabriella headed for her first class. It's ridiculous to feel disappointed that Troy wants to put together a band without me, she thought. After all, she was going to see him at lunch, and they were going to grab some pizza after school, and they had already made plans for next weekend . . . she was going to have plenty of chances to hang out with him.

So why, she wondered, do I suddenly feel so left out?

CHAPTER TWO

"Okay, guys, let's start with some drills," Troy called out. He was in the gym with the rest of the basketball team. They bounded on to the court, slapping high fives and grinning.

"Time to catch some Wildcat fever!" Chad yelled as he grabbed a ball and threw it to Jason Cross.

Jason spun and threw the ball to Zeke Baylor, who caught it easily and tossed it to Troy.

"Great job," Troy said. "Now, pick up the pace . . ."

As they practised their passing skills, they moved faster and faster. The ball spun through the air. No one dropped it, no one fumbled, no one missed a step – they were definitely in a groove today!

By the end of the drill, they were sweaty and happy. There was nothing like the feeling of working together as a team, Troy thought. They had been playing together for so long that they could anticipate each other's moves and get the ball to the right person at the right time without even thinking about it. It was as if they were all moving to the same rhythm, feeling the same beat, listening to the same drummer–

"I could be the drummer," Jason was saying.

Troy snapped to attention. "What did you say?"

Jason threw the ball to him and they started doing layup drills. "I said, I could be the drummer for the band. I could use my dad's drum kit. It's been sitting in the attic for about ten years, but I just need to dust it off and I'll be good to go."

"I can borrow my brother's bass," Zeke said eagerly.

Troy shot Chad a look.

"I guess I kinda told the guys our idea already," Chad said. "Sorry."

"Oh. Well, cool." Troy shrugged, trying to look casual. He thought he'd be the one to tell the guys; after all, it was his idea, wasn't it? But he knew Chad was excited about the band. It wasn't that big a deal that he'd told them.

"Hey, what are we going to call the band?" Chad said.

"I thought I'd come up with something tonight," Troy said. Of course, he had a lot of homework to do, but the band name was way too important to leave to the last minute–

" 'Cause I'm really good at things like coming up with band names!" Chad said, interrupting his thoughts.

Troy said, "Well, actually, I've already started brainstorming some ideas–"

"How about Blink 68–67?" Chad suggested

eagerly. "It's perfect, because we won the championship game, 68–67, and if you *blinked*, you would have missed it!"

"Um . . ." Troy said. "That's a little derivative, don't you think?"

Chad shrugged cheerfully. "Okay. If that name doesn't work, I've got a million more!"

"We'd better start thinking about our set list," Jason chimed in. "How many songs do we get to play in the competition?"

"I'm not sure," Troy answered. "I'll check when I sign us up and then we can talk about it–"

" 'Cause, dude, I totally think we should do 'We Are the Champions'! That's the most rockin' song ever! Not to mention *extremely* appropriate for members of the Wildcats basketball team!"

Troy shook his head. "I think we should pick something that people can dance to," he said. "Don't worry, I'll think of something. Now, c'mon, guys, we gotta focus on *basketball* right now."

“Yes, sir, captain, sir.” Chad saluted him with a grin and passed him the ball.

Troy dribbled downcourt and made a basket. *Swish!* Nothing but net!

He grinned. Now he felt like his old self: on top of his game and in control.

Basketball practice was in full swing in the gym while Gabriella was walking down the hall to room 154, feeling just a little nervous. A few weeks ago, the school counsellor had announced that she was organizing a peer-tutoring programme so that students who had a firm grasp of certain subjects could help others who were struggling.

At the time, Gabriella had thought that this would be the perfect extra-curricular activity for her. After all, she made straight As every semester, and she liked helping other students when they were struggling to understand something in class . . . so, in what she now considered a moment of madness, she had signed up.

Her forehead was creased with worry as she

approached the classroom where she would meet, for the first time, the person she had been assigned to tutor in algebra. What if the person didn't like her? What if she couldn't explain the maths concepts clearly? What if she tried her very best and still failed?

She bit her lip as she swung the door open . . . and saw Ryan Evans sitting at a desk, looking just as anxious as she felt.

"You're my tutor?" he asked, shocked. Sharpay, he thought, was going to freak when she found out that the girl who beat her to the lead role in the school musical was teaching him. True, she and Gabriella had come to an uneasy truce by the time *Twinkle Towne* ended its run, but Sharpay still had a chip on her shoulder about having *any* kind of competition in the world of showbiz – let alone *good* competition.

"I guess so." Gabriella decided to double-check. "Algebra two, right?"

"Yeah, that's me," he said dolefully. "I'm a complete dunce when it comes to maths."

"Oh, I'm sure that's not true." She smiled as she sat down next to him. "I mean, you're such a good singer!"

He eyed her suspiciously. "Yeah . . ." he said slowly, "but what does that have to do with maths?"

"Well, counting out beats is maths, right?" she said brightly, trying to sound self-assured. She had actually just wanted to boost Ryan's confidence, but now that she thought about it, his singing ability probably wasn't going to translate too well into solving equations.

Fortunately, Ryan really *didn't* know much about algebra. He looked happy and relieved at her reasoning. "That's true!" he cried. "I never thought about it that way before!"

Gabriella nodded earnestly. "And if you can remember all the steps to a complicated dance routine, you can certainly remember algebraic formulas!"

"That's an *excellent* point." Ryan was totally with her now. I don't know why Sharpay thinks

Gabriella is so irritating, he thought. She seems really nice.

"And if you can figure out how to do choreography with ten dancers when three of them are left-handed, two of them can't kick above their waists and four of them are klutzes, then handling variables should be a breeze!" Gabriella concluded brightly.

"Oh, um . . . really?" Ryan looked unsure, and she realized that she had lost him by introducing variables into the metaphor.

"Absolutely!" she said, with as much conviction as she could muster. "But we're getting ahead of ourselves. Why don't we take a look at the work you're doing now . . ."

An hour later, Gabriella had led Ryan through a torturous word problem involving two cars travelling at different rates of speed from opposite directions. He finally understood how to solve the problem when she changed the storyline a bit, explaining that car A was packed with costumes for a play at a local dinner theatre, while car B's passengers were heading to an audition.

"I think the answer is, um, two hours?" Ryan said.

"Awesome!" Gabriella exclaimed, breathing a private sigh of relief. "You're absolutely right!"

"I . . . I am?" He looked stunned. "Are you sure? I'm hardly ever right. At least, that's what Sharpay says–"

"Yes, I'm sure! See, algebra's not so hard once you break it down."

"Not the way you explain it," he said. "It seems to make so much more sense than when Mrs Jefferson tries to teach it."

"Well, that's what peer tutoring is all about, right? Getting some help, one-on-one . . ." Gabriella glanced at her watch. "Oh, no, it's already five o'clock! I'm sorry, I've got to go. Troy and I are going to get some pizza."

"Oh, sure." Ryan looked disappointed. "Hey,

are you and Troy going to enter the Battle of the Bands? Sharpay said you probably would . . ."

A shadow passed over her face, but she said brightly, "No, I think Troy's going to do something with some of his friends from the team."

Hmm, Ryan thought. Sharpay will be very interested to hear that!

But Gabriella was asking him a question . . .

"So what do you and Sharpay have planned?"

"Nothing," he said, disgruntled. "Well, *Sharpay* has something planned. She wants to form a girl group." He gave a snort of disgust. "Like *that's* going to get a lot of votes!"

"Oh, well," she said philosophically, "we can't all be stars all the time, I guess."

Ryan's mouth hung open in shock. What was she saying? *We. Can't. All. Be. Stars . . . ?*

But before he could respond, she had turned on her PDA. "Hmm . . . how about meeting next Wednesday?"

"Great." Ryan smiled. He had been feeling so lonely today and had been dreading this tutoring session so much, but it had actually worked out well. Very well, in fact. "I'll be *counting* the days." He waited a second. "Get it? Counting the days?"

"Oh!" Gabriella did her best to laugh. "Very funny. Well, I gotta run! See you later!"

CHAPTER THREE

The next morning, Troy went to the school office to sign up his band for the competition. As he entered, he saw Sharpay carefully writing her name on the sign-up sheet in her usual huge, loopy handwriting. He peered over her shoulder.

"Are you sure everyone can read your name, Sharpay?" he asked, deadpan. "You might want to make it a little bigger."

She tossed her head in exasperation, her blonde hair flying. "You're always making jokes,

Troy, but this time I will have the last laugh! People are going to be stunned by my group's performance! You and your . . . *Neanderthal basketball players* don't stand a chance."

Troy had only been teasing, but he didn't like the way she sneered when she said "Neanderthal basketball players". It sounded as if she thought they weren't in her league, musically speaking – or that there was something wrong with basketball players. Or Neanderthals, for that matter.

"Hey, listen, we are going to *rock the house*!" he said, trying to inject a note of confident bravado into his voice.

"Oh, yes, I'm sure you will," Sharpay said with a poisonously sweet smile. "But this isn't about making a lot of noise. It's about talent – and I . . . that is, *my group*, has that in spades!"

"Oh, yeah?" Troy eyed her suspiciously. "Who else is in your group, anyway?"

She hesitated, then said, "That's a secret for right now. But believe me, we are going to win!

In fact–" she turned to Ms Dermot, the school secretary, who had been watching Troy and Sharpay's argument with amazement, "–you might want to keep that sign-up sheet with my autograph. It's going to be worth a lot some day!"

She flounced out of the office. Troy watched her go, wondering what she had planned . . .

Sharpay's plan was actually quite simple. Find three other girls who could sing on key, master simple choreography and be willing to stand behind her onstage, singing nothing but, "Oh, yeah" and "Mmm-hmm" without complaining. She already had Alicia and Charlotte, of course – face it, she had them at hello – but she needed one more girl to complete the group.

As she walked down the hall, she passed the choir room. Inside, the school choir was already practising for the holiday concert. As they swung into a spirited version of "Here Comes Santa Claus," Sharpay smirked. Choir was all right if you wanted to sing with 50 other people, she thought. But for gifted performers like herself, who should always be singing solo, it was just too, too . . . *anonymous.*

Even as she had that thought, the bell rang and the members of the choir came pouring out of the door, chattering among themselves as they headed for their next class. Sharpay pushed her way into the room, where she spotted the choir teacher.

"Excuse me!" she called out officiously. "Excuse me! I need to talk to you!"

Mrs Jones raised her eyebrows at this pushy girl, but she nodded. "Can I help you?"

"My name is Sharpay Evans." Sharpay waited for the woman to realize who she was.

Mrs Jones merely gave her an inquiring look. "Yes?"

"Well, I wanted . . . that is, I just wondered–" Sharpay floundered as she spoke. She couldn't believe Mrs Jones didn't know who she was! She took a deep breath and started again. "I'm putting together a girl group for the Battle of the

Bands," she explained. "I have two backing singers, but I need another one." Her gaze swept dismissively over the choir room. "I'm sure at least *one* of your singers will meet my standards."

"Ah, I see." The teacher nodded. "I'm sure I can recommend someone of the right . . . level for what you want," she added, hiding a smile. "In fact, I think Taylor McKessie would be *perfect.*"

"Taylor? Really?" Sharpay squinted into the distance, trying to bring Taylor to mind. Ah, yes. Beautiful. Brainiac. Boring. "She can sing?"

"I think you'll find her talent quite acceptable," the teacher said solemnly. She gave Sharpay a little wink.

"Oh, great!" Sharpay was relieved. There was no chance she'd be upstaged by someone whose talent was merely acceptable. "She sounds just right."

The teacher nodded. "I'm sure she will be." As Sharpay headed out of the door, she called out, "Good luck!"

Sharpay gave her a disdainful smile. As if luck

had anything to do with winning, she thought smugly.

Taylor was hunched over a lab table in chemistry, rereading her scrawled notes as she waited for class to begin. She really didn't need to refresh her memory – she was already reading ahead in the textbook just for fun – but she wanted to get her mind off that disastrous choir practice.

The choir teacher had warned her about letting her voice overpower the other singers. "You have a powerful instrument," Mrs Jones had told her privately, soon after she joined the choir.

"And that's bad?" Taylor was confused.

"No, no, it's good – if the rest of the singers could match it," Mrs Jones had explained. "But their singing just isn't as strong, so your voice throws the whole choir out of balance."

"Oh." Taylor always thought she had a good voice. Now she was beginning to wonder if she actually sounded like a braying donkey when she sang.

Mrs Jones had smiled at her kindly. "I'm sure I'll be able to give you a solo at some point. I just have to wait a while, since you're so new to the choir. Then you'll be able to let loose! But in the meantime, if you wouldn't mind exercising a little restraint?"

Taylor had nodded glumly. And she had tried, she really had. But in today's rehearsal, Mrs Jones still had to warn her three times to tone it down a bit. She had seen a few of the choir members exchange meaningful looks – a raised eyebrow here, a roll of the eyes there – and she had bitten her lip with embarrassment. She suspected that they all thought she was some kind of diva, which was so absolutely not true! She would never demand attention, fight for the spotlight or upstage someone else! She would never, for example, be like Sharpay –

"Hey, Taylor!"

Taylor jumped. Sharpay was standing in front of her lab table, smiling.

"What are you doing here?" Taylor asked. No

one would ever expect to see Sharpay in the advanced chemistry class! Taylor almost felt that she had conjured up the drama princess through her own thoughts . . .

"I'm here to offer you an incredible opportunity!" Sharpay cried.

"And what is that?" Taylor asked cautiously. The girl sounded like a salesperson, pitching a dubious and shady scheme. "A once-in-a-lifetime chance to invest in your next musical?"

"No, silly! Although–" Sharpay looked thoughtful, "–that's not a bad idea . . ."

Taylor sighed. What was the use of sarcasm if it flew right over the victim's head? "Sharpay, class is about to start. If you don't want to be trapped here figuring out the pH balance of different liquids, tell me what you want."

"Okay, listen. I'm putting together a girl group for the Battle of the Bands. I'll be lead singer, of course, but I need some really talented backing singers. I asked Mrs Jones for recommendations, and she said you would be perfect!

So . . ." Sharpay paused for a breath. "What do you think?"

"Mrs Jones recommended me? Really?"

Sharpay nodded. Taylor sat still for a minute, thinking hard. Mrs Jones had seen how difficult it was for her to hold back in her singing today. Maybe she thought Taylor needed practice staying in the background? Maybe she thought she needed to learn to blend in a little more? Maybe she was trying to tell Taylor that she shouldn't be thinking of solos just yet, that she had to earn the chance to sing the lead? Taylor felt chastened. Mrs Jones, she thought, is trying to teach me to be humble. That's the only reason she could have suggested that I sing backup behind someone like Sharpay!

Well, Taylor took pride in her willingness to learn the lessons she needed in order to succeed. She was not an egotistical airhead like some people she could mention! It would be tough to stand in the background and support Sharpay, but she knew it would be good for her in the long run. Taylor nodded to herself, her decision made.

"All right," she said to Sharpay, gritting her teeth. "I'll do it."

Sharpay's eyes widened in an expression of delight that could have been seen from the back balcony, had she actually been onstage. "Wonderful!" she exclaimed.

At that moment, Gabriella rushed in and pulled a lab stool up to the table. "Whew, can't believe I made it before the bell!" she said. She looked at Sharpay and Taylor as she pulled a notebook out of her rucksack. "So, what's so wonderful?"

"Taylor's joining my group for the Battle of the Bands," Sharpay said smugly.

"Really?" Gabriella gave her friend a questioning look. "That's . . . um . . . great."

"I'll explain later," Taylor whispered. She turned to Sharpay. "Hey, maybe Gabriella could join, too! She has an awesome voice–"

"Sorry, no." Sharpay's smile was strained.

"It's a four-girl group. You're the fourth girl."

"Would it be so hard to make it a five-girl group?" Taylor asked. This would be so much more fun if Gabriella were involved . . .

There was a brief, awkward silence.

"That's okay," Gabriella said quickly. "I'm really busy right now, anyway. You know, studying for the SAT, peer tutoring, all that stuff."

Sharpay smiled more warmly. "Well, this works out perfectly then, doesn't it?" She gave Taylor a little wave as she said, "First rehearsal tomorrow after school, in the choir room. I'll give you your music then. See you!"

As Sharpay flounced out of the room, Gabriella said, "*You* are singing backup for Sharpay?"

Taylor sighed. "Long story. I'll tell you after class."

Chemistry class finished right before lunch. Gabriella and Taylor took their sandwiches to a table outside and sat down.

"So?" Gabriella said. "What's going on? I can't believe you joined Sharpay's group!"

"Yeah, I know." Taylor started to carefully disassemble the healthy turkey sandwich – filled with lettuce, tomatoes and beansprouts – that her mother insisted on making for her at least three times a week. "That girl is whacked out! But Mrs Jones is an awesome choir director, so when I found out that she recommended me, I figured she must have a good reason." She shrugged and looked down, concentrating on the task of rebuilding her sandwich with just the bread and turkey slices.

"Mmm." Gabriella frowned at the leftover pile of veggies. "Well, I'm sure it will be a lot of fun."

Taylor looked at her questioningly. "You're not upset, are you? About not being in the group?"

"Oh, of course not!" Gabriella said airily. "I mean, Sharpay and I get along okay now, but it would still be pretty awkward to be singing with her. Plus, if I sang in her group, I'd be competing against Troy and, well . . ." She blushed, and Taylor gave her a knowing look.

"Uh-huh," Taylor said. "So what's the latest with you and that boy?"

"Well, since you *ask* . . ." Gabriella smiled and devoted the next hour to giving her friend a minute-by-minute description of the bike ride they took last weekend and discussing what kind of dress she should buy for the prom.

CHAPTER FOUR

"Okay, guys, let's get started!" Troy had to raise his voice to be heard over the cacophony that was being produced on the auditorium stage of East High School. Apparently, he didn't raise it enough.

Jason was banging away on his dad's drum kit. He seemed to be particularly fond of hitting the cymbals. Zeke was plunking with great enthusiasm – but no real skill – at his bass guitar. Chad was recreating the most awesome riffs from his favourite heavy metal bands. He actually sounded pretty good, Troy thought. But loud. Very, very loud.

"Guys!" Troy yelled. "Hey!"

Still no reaction. Finally, he put two fingers in his mouth and blew an ear-piercing whistle. Everyone stopped playing to look at him in surprise.

"Hey, dude, we're not in basketball practice right now," Chad said.

"Oh, yeah." Troy shuffled his feet, embarrassed. "Sorry about that. I just thought we should discuss a few things before we start playing–"

"Jammin'," Zeke said firmly. "We're not just playing, man. We're *jammin'*."

"Oh, yeah, right." Troy picked up his guitar. "But before we get started, um, jamming, maybe we should talk about a few things? Like what song we're going to play and–"

"–and the name of the band!" Chad shouted. "I got another one! New Kidz on the Court!"

"Too girly," Zeke objected.

"Yeah, sounds like a boy band," Jason agreed.

"Okay," Chad said, undaunted, "how about the Mighty Mighty B'Ball Tones? No? Well, what about No Foul–"

As the other boys continued to argue, Troy sighed and strummed a few lonely chords on his guitar.

"Okay, everyone, let's get started!" Sharpay clapped her hands. "Quiet, please!"

Alicia and Charlotte instantly fell silent. Taylor raised one eyebrow at Sharpay's high-handed attitude, but then she shrugged. Sharpay was the leader of this group, after all. She could run it the way she wanted.

"Thank you. Now, here is your music." Sharpay began passing out pages of sheet music. "I thought we would sing 'Stop! In the Name of Love'. It's a real old-school song from like, I don't know, the sixties–"

"1965," Taylor said helpfully. "Originally sung by The Supremes. It went to number one in the charts and it was nominated for a Grammy . . ."

"Oh, right." Sharpay stared at her for a long, displeased moment.

"Good choice." Taylor offered peaceably and Sharpay relaxed.

"Thanks. So I'll give you a few minutes to go over your score and then we can give it a try!"

The other girls obediently began flipping through their music, mouthing the words as they did so. Taylor pretended to look at hers, though she didn't need to. Her mother loved sixties music, so she had grown up singing these songs. She hummed a bit, smiling. This could actually be fun . . .

"Now, I've figured out exactly what kind of costumes we're going to wear," Sharpay said. She quickly passed out photocopies of sketches she had created the night before. The costumes were black miniskirts, white halter tops, white knee-high boots and huge, white earrings. Every girl's hair was teased into a bouffant hairdo.

Taylor nodded in appreciation. "Groovy."

Sharpay gave her a warm smile. "Thanks, Taylor! I want us to look and sing just like The Supremes – only better!"

Taylor raised one eyebrow. Better than The Supremes? Talk about setting the bar high.

"Um, Sharpay?" Alicia said timidly. "Who are The Supremes?"

Taylor was so shocked that she didn't wait for Sharpay to answer. "Only the best girl group of all time!" she cried. "They were one of the biggest acts in Motown! They had 12 number-one hits in the sixties, like 'Baby Love' and 'You Can't Hurry Love'! Not to mention–"

But Sharpay's eyes were glinting at her again. Too late, Taylor closed her mouth.

"Thank you for that history lesson, Taylor," she said icily. "But I think it's time we started rehearsing *our* song, don't you?" Sharpay turned on a boom box and began singing along to the music.

Give the girl credit, Taylor thought. She's giving a full-on performance, even though there are only three people listening. If nothing else, she's committed to her art.

Sharpay made a gesture for the other girls to come in with the backing vocals. They started singing, a little raggedly in Charlotte's case, and Sharpay smiled. Her voice got louder, and the backing singers swayed and doo-wopped away.

Taylor was in the groove, feeling fine, when she suddenly noticed that everyone else had stopped singing. They were all staring at her.

"Umm . . . what?" She had a sinking feeling in her stomach.

"Wow!" Alicia said, wide-eyed. "You're really good!"

"Good? You're awesome!" Charlotte added.

"Yes." Sharpay could barely squeeze the word out through her clenched teeth. "I had no idea, Taylor, what a big voice you have."

"Sorry. I'll try to tone it down," Taylor said sheepishly.

"Do that." Sharpay's words were clipped and icy. "Now, let's start again. From the top . . ."

CHAPTER FIVE

When Gabriella walked into room 154 for the next tutoring session, she found Ryan already there. He was dancing in front of the blackboard to the accompaniment of a song he was singing. The drama teacher, Ms Darbus, was sitting in the front row of desks watching him apprais-ingly.

Gabriella stopped, confused. She was sup-posed to be tutoring him, wasn't she? She checked her watch. Yes, it was time for their appointment. But why was Ms Darbus here? And why was Ryan singing "Stop! In the Name of Love"? And why was he *dancing*?

Ryan caught sight of Gabriella, but he didn't stop out of embarrassment, as most kids would have. Instead, he finished with a dramatic flourish, spinning around a few times and ending with both hands pointing at Gabriella. She applauded weakly, because he clearly expected her to. Ms Darbus stood up, applauding wildly and yelling, "Bravo!"

"Thanks, Ms Darbus!" he said, a little out of breath. He turned to Gabriella and asked, "What do you think? Pretty spectacular, huh?"

"Yeah, it's, um . . . spectacular, all right," she echoed. That seemed to be the safest response.

It worked. He grinned and said, "I'm working up some choreography for Sharpay's group."

"Oh, that's great!" Gabriella said sincerely. She knew he had been feeling left out.

He shrugged. "Not as great as singing onstage. But Sharpay always talks about how even the little people behind the scenes have their role to play in making someone a star." He sighed deeply. "I just never thought that *I* would be one of the little people."

"Yeah, I know," she said wistfully.

He cocked his head to one side, puzzled. "What do you mean? After your performance in *Twinkle Towne*, you became a star! *You* would never be forced to sit backstage, watching while other selfish people stole the spotlight for themselves using some egotistical ploy–"

"I wouldn't be too sure of that," she interrupted, sensing that he was working his way into a full-blown tantrum. "I mean, not that I care, really, but I'm not singing in the Battle of the Bands either."

Ms Darbus had been listening to their conversation in silence. Now she stepped forward, her eyes flashing.

"That is utterly absurd!" she cried.

"Um . . . excuse me?" Gabriella said.

"A singer of your talent is not going to be

represented in the Battle of the Bands? Ridiculous!"

Gabriella smiled at the compliment, then shook her head. "Well, it *is* called the Battle of the Bands," she pointed out. "I wasn't asked to join a band, so–"

"What about Troy's band?" Ryan said. "Can't you join that?"

She shrugged. "He's playing with his basketball buddies. It's a chance for them to . . . you know . . . bond. I wouldn't want to get in the way of that."

"Oh." Ryan looked at her with the heartfelt sympathy of another supremely talented person who has been unfairly overlooked. "That's too bad."

"No, no, it's fine!" Gabriella did her best to give a carefree laugh. "There are always other chances to sing, right?"

"Right." Ryan didn't sound convinced.

"Wrong!" Ms Darbus snapped. "Read the rules of the competition more closely. The Battle of the Bands is open to any group or *singer* who wants to enter. And you, Ms Montez, are a singer. Now, I want you to march right down to the office and sign up for a solo. Now."

"But, but, but–" Gabriella stammered.

Ryan's eyes were alight with excitement. "You'll be the only solo singer! You'll stand out! You might even win!"

"But I don't want to stand out–"

"Nonsense!" Ms Darbus waved away her protest. "A girl of your talent shouldn't be in the audience, applauding other people! You should be onstage, basking in others' applause!"

"Thank you, but I–"

Ms Darbus clapped her hands in glee. "Good! Then it's decided! You don't even have to go to the office. I'm going to a meeting with Principal Matsui, so I'll sign you up while I'm there. And I'll ask Kelsi Neilsen to be your accompanist. I know she'll be glad to help out. Now, the only question left is what you should sing – but I'm sure I'll come up with something by tomorrow."

"I'm not sure–" Gabriella said weakly, trying in vain to backtrack from the commitment she had somehow just made to compete in the Battle of the Bands.

"Of course you're not! That's why Ryan and I are here to urge you on." Ms Darbus said.

Ryan nodded enthusiastically. "You'll be great, Gabriella," he said.

She smiled, softened by his obvious sincerity. "Well . . . all right."

"Excellent! Come by my classroom at noon tomorrow and we'll begin working!" the drama teacher said. "Until then!"

She swept out of the room. Ryan and Gabriella stared at each other, a little surprised and shocked by what had just happened. Ryan grinned at her. "You're going to be so great!" he said, excited.

"Well, we'll see," she answered, but her eyes were sparkling. "Now, we'd better get to work," she said firmly. "Let's start with the problems on page 32 . . ."

* * *

"Hey, Troy!" Gabriella smiled as she called out from backstage.

Troy and his band had just finished a disastrous attempt at a hard-rocking remake of "Twist and Shout". He smiled back when he saw her, but he was clearly distracted. "Oh, hi, Gabriella."

He turned to the band. "Let's take five, okay, guys?"

They nodded and started chatting as Troy walked over to her. "I'm sorry, I can't talk long. I think we're going to have to rehearse for a while longer."

"Oh." Her smile dimmed. "I thought we were going to catch a movie–"

"I know, I know." He sighed. "I'd like to, but we really need the practice."

"Of course," she said, putting a hand on his arm. "I totally understand. Especially since–"

"Yes?" he asked.

Gabriella bit her lip. She had wanted to tell him about singing a solo in the competition, but this just wasn't the moment. He was barely able to pay any attention to her at all! "Oh, nothing," she said, just as Zeke ran up.

"I'm getting a soda," Zeke said. "You guys want anything?"

"No, thanks," Troy said. "Hey, don't be too long, okay? We have a lot of work to do."

Zeke pointed at Troy and winked. "No worries, bro. I'll be back in a flash!"

As he ran out of the door, Troy sighed and turned back to Gabriella. "Sorry about that," he said. "We haven't started on time yet and . . . anyway. What were you saying?"

She brightened up a bit. "Oh, well, I was going to tell you that–"

"Hey, Gabriella, did you hear that last song?" Chad called out. "How did we sound? Awesome, right?"

"I just caught the end of it. You guys sound really–" she hesitated; '*good*' wasn't exactly the right word, "–like you've been working hard," she finished tactfully.

"Yeah!" Jason nodded eagerly. "We'll have this song nailed in a couple of days."

"I don't know about that . . ." Troy looked sceptical.

"Okay, maybe a week," Jason admitted. "At the most."

Troy ran his hand through his hair in frustration. "It's not just playing the song," he said. "We gotta look like a rock band! But all we do is stand on the stage, like our feet are glued in one place."

Zeke returned with his can of soda, but found the other boys looking downcast. "You're right," Chad said. "It's a lot easier to jump around when you're playing air guitar. But, man, with a real guitar – you gotta play all the right notes in the right order and everything!"

Jason and Zeke nodded in agreement.

"Well, we have to figure this out," Troy said, feeling a little lost. "Somehow." If this were basketball, he thought, we could run drills. But what kind of drills do you run in order to look like real rockers?

Gabriella cleared her throat. "Um . . . could I make a suggestion?"

They all turned to look at her.

"Yeah, sure," Zeke said. "We need help! Any kind of help!"

"Well, Ryan Evans told me that he's doing choreography for Sharpay's group–"

The boys all looked uneasily at each other.

"I don't know if we want, um . . . *choreography*," Chad said.

"Yeah, we need something more like . . . like *moves*, you know?" Zeke chimed in.

"But that's what choreography *is*!" Gabriella cried. "And Ryan really is very good."

"Would he help us?" Troy asked. "I mean, Sharpay pretty much calls the shots, right? She won't be happy about anything that will give us an advantage."

Gabriella shrugged. "I don't know. But it wouldn't hurt to ask . . ."

The boys hesitated, then nodded. As they started discussing who should approach Ryan,

Gabriella decided that she could always tell Troy about her decision to enter the Battle of the Bands later – when he had more time to focus on her instead of the band.

Troy tucked the idea of talking to Ryan in the back of his mind and didn't think about it for a few days. Then he and the guys showed up in the auditorium to rehearse, only to find that Sharpay and her singers were already on the stage!

"Okay, everyone," she said bossily to Taylor, Alicia and Charlotte. "Line up behind me. No – farther back. I'm going to need at least three feet between us, right, Ryan?"

Ryan was standing to one side, arms folded, watching them critically. "At least," he agreed. "You're going to have to spin around, then do a couple of high kicks – three feet is the minimum amount of clearance you'll need. Five feet might be better."

Alicia and Charlotte quickly scooted back a few feet, but Taylor stood her ground. "There's going to be a curtain across the back of the stage, right?" she said. "We'll run into it if we back up five feet–"

Sharpay waved a dismissive hand. "We'll figure that out in dress rehearsal," she said breezily. "Now, back, back . . ."

Troy stepped forward. "Excuse me," he said.

"Oh, hi, Troy!" Sharpay gave him a big smile. "I'm so excited about the Battle of the Bands, aren't you?"

"Um, sure. But there's something we need to discuss–" Troy began.

"I mean, I know we're competitors and everything, but that doesn't mean we can't be *friendly* competitors, does it?" she purred.

"Absolutely not." Troy nodded agreeably. "Winning some trophy isn't really the point, anyway, right? This is about having fun and raising money for the new tennis courts."

Winning wasn't the point? Sharpay's smile slipped for a moment in confusion, but she recovered quickly. "You are so right, Troy," she went on. "You and I think *so* much alike! But that makes sense, doesn't it, since we have so much in common? We both have a musical vision, of course. And *I'm* the musical leader of *my* incredible singing group, and *you're* in charge of your–" she glanced at Chad, Zeke and Jason, and smiled condescendingly, "–little band."

Troy just grinned. No chance of getting a big ego around Sharpay, he thought. She would always be able to cut you down to size.

But the other boys took her remark more personally.

"Dude, who is she calling a little band?" Zeke muttered to Jason. "She makes us sound like The Wiggles."

Jason shook his head in disbelief. "We're not little," he muttered back. "We're hardcore."

Troy said to Sharpay, "Yeah, but see, the thing is . . . we booked the stage from four to six." He glanced at his watch and added, "It's 4:05. So . . ."

"So . . . you must have got the time wrong," she said, tossing her hair. "*We* booked it from three to seven. And we're not giving it up."

Okay, Troy thought. So much for friendly competition.

"No way we got our time wrong," Chad said. "I stopped by the office myself to sign us up!"

"Oh?" she said disdainfully. "So you can actually write?"

Ryan, Alicia and Charlotte simpered at her wisecrack.

"Anyway," she went on, "we're all set up now, so it makes more sense for you to come back another time. Let's see, I have the room reserved until seven o'clock, but I don't want to be unreasonable . . . how about if you come back at, oh, say, 6:55?"

"Oh?" Chad said, mimicking her tone. "So you can actually tell the time?"

Zeke and Jason cracked up. Troy tried to keep a straight face, but he couldn't help smiling just a little.

"Look," he said reasonably, "maybe we can compromise–"

Sharpay's chin lifted an inch. Ryan shuddered. He knew what it meant when she lifted her chin . . .

"No compromise," she said icily. "Rules are rules. I signed up for four hours, and I am going to rehearse for four hours!"

"But, Sharpay, isn't that a little . . . extreme?" Troy ran his hands through his hair in frustration. "We only have three weeks until the Battle of the Bands!" He gave her a winning smile. "Couldn't you cut your rehearsal short, just this one time?"

Sharpay tilted her head to look at him. She relaxed a tiny bit. A small smile even tugged at her lips. "Well," she said, "since you're asking so nicely–"

"And the Troy Bolton charm works again!" Chad muttered to Jason, who laughed and gave him a high five.

Unfortunately, Sharpay heard the comment as well. Her face darkened. Did they think she could be manipulated by a boyish grin and a winsome manner? She had been in show business a long, long time – long enough to know all about back-stage plotting and duplicitous, two-faced, sneaky charmers who just wanted to get their own way!

So she straightened her spine and gave Troy Bolton and his buddies her best diva glare. "Forget it!" Sharpay snapped. "We are going to use our full rehearsal time. And when it's time for the competition, we'll see who has true talent and who needs to go back to playing air guitar! In fact, I want to put you and your band on notice. We are going to *take you down.*"

Troy stood up a little straighter at that. He had wanted to be easygoing about all this, but her challenge had just kicked his competitive spirit into high gear. Forget about friendly competition, he thought. Forget about just having fun and not caring about trophies and all that peace-and-love nonsense.

After all, this competition was called the *Battle* of the Bands and Troy Bolton knew one thing about battles: the goal was to win.

CHAPTER SIX

After the showdown in the auditorium, Troy really didn't want to approach Ryan for help of any kind at any time. But three rehearsals later, he had to face facts. They needed help. Now.

He caught up with Ryan after study hall. "Hey, can I talk to you for a sec?" Troy asked.

Ryan looked around wildly, searching the corridor for someone, *anyone* else Troy could be talking to, but everybody had vanished into their classrooms.

"Who, me?" he said weakly.

Ryan's mouth twitched as he looked at Troy. The poor guy looks like a scared rabbit, Troy thought. He didn't see how Ryan could possibly help the band, but Gabriella had seemed pretty sure, so . . . "Yeah, you." He jerked his head toward an empty classroom. "In here."

They stood by the blackboard, facing each other warily. "Okay, I know this is weird," Troy said, "but the guys and I . . . well, we need some help with our band."

Ryan shook his head, confused. "You're playing rock 'n' roll," he said. "All I know about are show tunes."

"Yeah, I know. We don't need help with the music. Or–" he added honestly, "–not much, anyway. But we definitely need help with . . . well, *looking* like a rock band. You know what I mean?"

"Oh, yeah." Ryan nodded knowingly. "Appearances are half the battle! If not more!"

"Right, so, here's the thing . . ." Troy hesitated,

then plunged ahead. "Would you be willing to coach us a little?"

Ryan's eyes widened in shock. "Coach?" he said, astonished. "You?" He glanced around, wondering if perhaps people were hiding in the supply closet, just waiting for him to take the bait. "Is this a trick?"

"No, I really mean it. I think you could help us. A lot," Troy said. "Look, I know it might seem a little weird, considering how competitive we were during auditions for the musical. But there were no hard feelings in the end, right?"

"Nooo," Ryan said slowly. "Not really." Although, he thought, Sharpay had taken a vow to win the lead in next year's musical, no matter what. And when Sharpay said "no matter what" – as Ryan knew from bitter experience – there was only one thing to do. *Back away slowly . . .*

"And dude, let's face it – you're an awesome dancer!"

Ryan's eyes narrowed with suspicion as he

tried to work out what was happening here. For some reason, Gabriella's algebra lessons flashed through his mind, and he started imagining an equation that would explain this bizarre moment in his life:

[Troy Bolton, basketball star] +
[compliment on Ryan's dancing] -
[any apparent sarcasm] = X

So that meant that X was . . . ?

Ryan shook his head. No, it was no use. This just did not compute.

"And that dance you and Sharpay did for the musical audition . . . " Troy was going on. "That was great. Lots of rhythm, lots of flash – exactly what my band needs more of."

Hmm, Ryan thought. Troy didn't sound as if he was making fun of Ryan. In fact, he sounded . . . well . . . sincere.

Ryan stood a little taller. "It's true. In fact, I think that routine was a major breakthrough for my work–" Then he felt a sudden wave of panic roll over him. *No! What was he thinking?*

Was he insane? There was no way he could do this!

He whispered in a worried voice, "The only thing is . . . well, my sister–"

Troy held up his hands. "Say no more. I totally get it."

Ryan smiled with relief. Of course, Troy knew all about Sharpay. He would be the first person to understand why Ryan couldn't possibly help Troy's band, no matter how much they undoubtedly needed his talent, vision and energy . . .

"We'll be sure to cover your tracks," Troy went on. "So can we start tomorrow afternoon?"

Ryan's smile faded. He didn't remember agreeing to Troy's plan, but apparently he had. He felt a flutter of nerves in his stomach. "Sharpay will be really, really mad–" he began.

"She'll never find out," Troy said confidently. He winked at Ryan. "Trust me."

As Troy was talking to Ryan, Gabriella had slipped into the empty choir room. She walked slowly around the room, remembering the times that she and Troy had rehearsed here for the musical auditions. It had been so much fun, and they had connected so well, and she had felt so free and fearless as she sang with him . . .

How in the world had she ever let Ms Darbus talk her into singing a solo?

She slumped down in a chair, her head in her hands.

"Gabriella?"

She looked up to see Kelsi looking at her shyly, a sheaf of music clutched in her arms.

"Are you okay?" Kelsi asked.

Gabriella laughed a little and shrugged. "Oh, yeah, I guess. I'm just having a sudden attack of ultimate stage fright – and I haven't even started practising my song yet!"

Kelsi smiled and waved away her fears with a jaunty flip of the hand. "Oh, don't worry about that! Ms Darbus and I picked out a perfect song for you to sing. It's called 'These Boots Are Made for Walkin'.' You're going to love it!"

Gabriella sat up straight. Despite her misgivings, she felt a wave of confidence surge through her at Kelsi's words. "Really? Because I've never sung a solo before and–"

"Nothing to it!" Kelsi sat at the piano and placed her fingers on the keys. "Now, let's get started . . ."

The next afternoon, Ryan slipped into the auditorium wearing sunglasses, plain black tracksuit bottoms, a black jersey and a black baseball cap pulled down low over his forehead. He was thanking his lucky stars that Sharpay's band was not rehearsing until later that day. In fact, she was, at this very moment, across town in her weekly tap dance class, but she would be back at school in a few hours to rehearse with her group. And she had made it clear that he had to be there as well, to start teaching them their moves.

Ryan thought he had just enough time to work on some fundamentals with Troy's band and maybe get a bite to eat before Sharpay came back.

The most important thing, of course, was to avoid detection. Ryan knew he was taking a risk, but he thought he could pull it off. All he had to do was keep his head down and stay as inconspicuous as possible–

"Hey, Ryan!" Chad yelled from across the auditorium. Ryan jumped. "What's up, man?"

"Shhh!" Ryan hissed. "Keep your voice down!"

Zeke and Jason slammed through the auditorium doors, jostling each other and joking around.

"There he is, the Man in Black!" Zeke yelled. "What's up with the cat-burglar outfit?"

"Yeah, a person might think you were trying to hide or something," Jason teased. "Maybe from a certain ice princess named Sharpay?"

"Shh! Shh!" Ryan kept hissing. They didn't take the hint.

"Man, she's so frosty, we could throw her in the swimming pool and turn it into a hockey rink," Chad said.

The other boys howled with laughter.

"Hey, guys," Troy said as he walked in the door. He looked at Ryan. "The coast is clear, right?"

Ryan nodded. "For now," he said. "But Sharpay is going to be here in two hours and you guys better be gone. Long gone."

"We're not afraid of your sister, man!" Zeke protested.

"Really?" Ryan was surprised. "*I* am." He gave them a meaningful look. "Believe me, the closer we get to the Battle of the Bands, the more uptight she'll get. And when Sharpay gets uptight–"

Jason shuddered.

"Yeah, we got the point," Zeke said, nodding vigorously.

Troy clapped his hands. "Okay, then! Let's get started."

A few minutes later, Ryan was wondering just what he had got himself into.

"No, no, no!" he cried as Chad tried to do a

twist while playing a solo. "You've got to get down low! Keep your balance! Use your quads to twist back up!"

Chad frowned in concentration, tried to do all those things at once and promptly fell over.

Jason hit a jaunty rim shot on his cymbal to punctuate the moment.

There was a long silence. "Ow," Chad murmured to the floor.

Ryan sighed. "Okay, you can take five. Now, Zeke."

Zeke gulped. "Yes, sir?" He would never have thought he could be cowed by some little drama-club dweeb, but Ryan was even tougher in rehearsal than Troy was in basketball practice.

"You're standing in one place like you've put down roots," Ryan said. "I know the bass isn't the flashiest instrument, but try to move a little bit. Nod your head, shift from side to side . . . go ahead. Try it."

Zeke took a deep breath and started playing a bass beat while nodding his head.

After a few moments, Troy groaned. "Maybe it's better if he just stands there."

"Yeah, when I think about moving, I forget how to play," Zeke said sheepishly.

Ryan glared at them. "Unacceptable!" he snapped. "A professional keeps working and working until he can perform at the peak of his abilities."

"Yeah, but, see, that's the problem," Zeke explained. "I think this *is* the peak of my abilities."

"Today it is your peak," Ryan answered loftily. "But it will not be your peak tomorrow."

"That's real mystical, Ryan. I feel like I'm in a remake of *The Karate Kid*," Zeke muttered.

"No joke," Chad agreed.

Ryan clapped his hands sharply to get their attention. "You two, go to stage left and practise!"

Chad and Zeke looked around, clueless. Ryan sighed heavily and pointed. "Stage left is over there."

They moved away, relieved to have the pressure off for the moment. Ryan turned to Troy. "Now, let's see what you've got . . ."

After two hours, the rehearsal for Troy's band had ended. Ryan wiped his forehead, exhausted. He had never worked so hard in his life, he thought. He was going to have to spend a serious amount of time watching MTV; he needed *lots* of ideas if he was going to have any hope of making Troy's band look good! Maybe he should rent some DVDs of old rock bands like The Rolling Stones, too. This gig was turning into quite a challenge, but, in a way, he was enjoying being out of his element. And working with basketball players wasn't nearly as frightening as he had feared . . .

"Alicia! Charlotte! Taylor!" His sister's voice knifed through the auditorium. Startled, Ryan ducked behind some scenery that had been left onstage to be repainted. He couldn't let her see him – she was sure to ask all kinds of impossible questions, like *What are you doing up there onstage*? And his mind would go blank and he would start to stutter and she would be able to tell from the expression on his face that he was hiding something!

He heard her continue. "I told you we had to start rehearsal at six o'clock on the dot! Let me give you a showbiz motto: Punctual Equals Professional!"

"I'm so sorry, Sharpay, my mother insisted that I had to finish my homework before I came back to school, just because I happen to be failing geometry!" Alicia bleated as she ran down the aisle to the stage. "It will never happen again, I swear!"

"I would hope not," Sharpay huffed, her arms crossed in displeasure.

Ryan winced. He knew what that crossed-arms posture meant and it wasn't good. Carefully, he began edging his way through the forest of wooden tree cutouts, heading for the wings of the stage. As he inched along, feeling his way, he kept one wary eye focused on his sister.

She was now confronting Charlotte and Taylor, who were hurrying toward her, out of breath. "And what are your excuses?"

"My brother said he would drop me off, but he took forever to get ready!" Charlotte cried.

Sharpay nodded grandly, accepting the excuse like a queen accepting a petition for mercy from a lowly commoner. "In the future," she promised, "I will pick you up personally."

Charlotte's eyes widened in delighted surprise.

"Taylor?" Sharpay snapped. "Why are *you* late?"

Taylor's mouth was hanging open as she looked back and forth from one girl to the other. Was Sharpay serious? Did she really expect Taylor to grovel for forgiveness, just because she was a few minutes – okay, ten minutes – late for rehearsal?

Sharpay's eyes glittered dangerously.

Apparently, Taylor thought, the answer to that question was yes.

"Well–" she began. Before she could utter another word, there was a crash from the stage. The girls all turned to see a row of wooden trees falling forwards and bringing down the curtain with them, all in what seemed like slow motion.

Backstage, Ryan had his eyes squinched shut and his fingers in his ears. Oh no, oh no, oh no, now she'll catch me for sure, he thought.

But Sharpay was simply staring in shock at the mess of splintered scenery that now littered the stage. The stage on which she was about to sing and dance! The stage that was supposed to be clear for their rehearsal! She blinked, hardly able to take in the true extent of this tragedy.

As she stood there, rooted to the spot in horror, Ryan eased his way out of sight and fled to the side door.

A few moments later, he trotted through the main door of the auditorium, a huge, happy smile on his face.

"Hey, girls, are you ready to get busy?" he called out cheerfully. He came to a dramatic halt and stared at the stage, his mouth hanging open, dumbstruck. "Oh, my gosh!" he cried out. "What *happened*?"

As they all started telling him at once, he smiled to himself, relieved. Thank goodness for my excellent thespian training, he thought. It comes in handy at the oddest times . . .

CHAPTER SEVEN

Gabriella sat in the school library alone. She had several books spread out in front of her and was staring at her laptop. She sighed. Her essay on the Civil War wasn't due for weeks, but she thought it would be a good idea to get an early start. Usually, sitting at a library table and working would have made her feel happy, productive and in control.

Instead, she felt lonely, out of sorts and, well, a little jealous.

This is silly, she told herself. Just because Taylor didn't have time to hang out after school. They'd only planned to grab a soda and talk . . .

She shook her head at the thought and opened a book at random. She stared at the page with resolve. This was actually a perfect opportunity to get ahead in some of her classes, maybe even have a little less homework to do over the weekend.

She slammed the book shut, scowling. And that was another problem! What happened to the plans that she and Troy had made for this weekend? They had talked about going to the aquarium or taking a long bike ride or just hanging out and listening to music.

Then he had called her last night to say that he couldn't get together with her. "I'm sorry," he had said. "It's the band. It's just taking so much time–"

"Okay, I understand," she had replied, making her voice calm and reasonable. She had seen enough VH-1 specials to know how fans hated the evil girlfriend who makes the band break up. She wasn't going to be one of *them*. "So you're rehearsing all day Saturday? That's great! But what about Sunday? Maybe we could get together then?"

There had been a long, long pause. Gabriella felt her heart sink.

"I'm sorry," Troy had said. He had sounded sorry, too, unless, of course, he was just pretending . . . No. She would not let herself think that!

"I really want to see you," he went on. "But the band has such a long way to go and the concert is only a couple of weeks away! I mean, if you could hear the way Jason plays drums! Is it possible to be born with absolutely no sense of rhythm? I mean, *none at all*?"

She had laughed, as she knew he wanted her to and said all the right things about how important it was that the band perform at least well enough to avoid total humiliation. Then she agreed that they would go out for a celebration dinner when the Battle of the Bands was over.

But she had hung up the phone with tears in her eyes and she hadn't been able to concentrate on anything – not even something as undemanding as watching a TV reality show – all evening.

She frowned and flipped another page. And then today, Taylor had rushed up to her between classes and said, "Gabriella, I'm so sorry, but I can't meet you today after school!"

"Oh, okay." She had smiled, trying not to look disappointed. "What's up?"

Taylor had rolled her eyes sarcastically. "It's that Sharpay! She called a special rehearsal today. As if rehearsing four times a week isn't enough!"

"Oh. Well, I guess she just wants you guys to do the best you can," Gabriella had said, forcing herself to smile.

Taylor had shrugged. "Or she's psychotically driven to win every competition she enters," she suggested.

Gabriella had smiled at that, a real smile. "To*may*to, to*mah*to," she said and Taylor laughed.

So they ended on a good note. But now Taylor was in the choir room, singing, and Troy was in the auditorium, jamming with his buddies, and she was in the library, all alone.

"There you are!"

Gabriella jumped as Ms Darbus's voice rang out through the empty library. The drama teacher bustled up to her, all business. "What are you doing in this, this –" she looked around at the still, silent room, so different from the energy and excitement of the theatre and shuddered, "– this mausoleum?"

"Um . . . studying?" Gabriella said.

Ms Darbus's sharp eyes focused on her and narrowed meaningfully. "I think not," she said loftily. "In fact, *I* think you are hiding out."

Gabriella opened her mouth to protest, then closed it. Ms Darbus was absolutely right. "I guess I just miss my friends," she said weakly.

"This moping isn't like you, Gabriella," the teacher went on. "And speaking of friends . . . I believe I've noticed a couple of people helping you out in the last week, haven't I?"

Hmm. Gabriella frowned slightly as she considered this.

She had only rehearsed with Kelsi three times, but she loved the song and she already had the lyrics down cold. In her quiet way, Kelsi boosted her confidence more and more; each time they worked together, Kelsi gave her tips on singing better, but then finished each rehearsal by giving Gabriella a list of everything she had done well.

And Ryan had stayed an extra ten minutes after each tutoring session to show her a few simple movements she could do as she was singing. The choreography wasn't elaborate, but it was just enough to give her performance, as he said, "a smattering of the three *P*s – polish, professionalism, and *pizzazz*!"

Maybe, Gabriella thought, she should focus more on all the good stuff she was getting from the Battle of the Bands, instead of thinking about how much her feelings had been hurt . . .

She nodded with sudden certainty. "You're right, Ms Darbus."

"Of course I am," the teacher sniffed. "And I happened to see Kelsi sneaking into the choir room five minutes ago. If you hurry, you may be able to fit in one more practice after school today . . ."

"Got it." Gabriella grinned as she grabbed her books and headed for the door. "And . . . thanks."

Another week of rehearsals went by, which meant it was also a week filled with spats, frayed nerves and exploding tempers.

Ryan rushed into a rehearsal with Troy's band in the afternoon. First, he taught Troy and Chad a basic rock-star stance – neck of the guitar pointed at the sky, legs planted wide, head thrown back – then had them practise it over and over again while he worked with Jason on flipping his drumsticks during the song. Zeke had almost mastered the head bob, so Ryan had him move on to a more advanced stage (a slight shuffle back and forth). Then he went back to Troy and Chad, who were now working on their air jumps but landing incredibly awkwardly . . .

Before he knew it, the two hours were up and it was time to dash down the hall to the choir room. As he ran through the auditorium doors, he spotted Sharpay at the end of the hall. She seemed to have caught a glimpse of him – at least, her head had whipped around and her laser stare had practically pinned him to the wall!

He gulped, reversed direction and fled down the hall toward the gym. He skidded around a corner, darted through an empty classroom and out of a back exit, circled the school and raced through the front doors – where he found Sharpay standing in front of the choir room, looking at her watch and pointedly tapping her foot.

"You're late," she greeted him.

"Sorry," he said, panting. "Had . . . a few . . . errands . . . to run."

"Really." Her tone was glacial. "Was one of those errands in the auditorium, by any chance?"

He shook his head, too panic-stricken to speak.

"Because I could have sworn I saw you coming out of there five minutes ago–"

"Huh." He tried to think of something else to say, but as usual when facing his sister, nothing came to mind.

After a long moment, she shrugged. "Oh, well. At least you're finally here! Listen, you really need to work with the other girls. I've got my routine down cold, of course, but I can't have my backing singers falling all over themselves . . ."

As the Battle of the Bands competition got closer, Gabriella found that she was seeing even less of Troy and Taylor. For the past week, Troy had only been able to spare a few minutes before school, and she only managed to have lunch with Taylor once.

And every second she was with them, she had to listen to them talk about the competition. They told her their worries (they would never learn their songs on time, the other bands were probably much better, maybe they should have chosen a better song). They told her their complaints (the band was still arguing about names, the other backing singers couldn't stay on key, everyone wanted to choose a different song but couldn't they see it was way too late?). They told her their secret fears (they would forget the words of the song, they would trip trying to execute a dance step, people would laugh at them).

Gabriella tried to be a good friend and listen to all this with patience and understanding, but by the end of the week she was ready to snap. And, somehow, she had never found the right moment to interrupt and let them know that she was competing too. In fact, she had to admit to herself that there was a little part of her that didn't want to tell them, that liked imagining how shocked they would be when she stepped out on the stage by herself. She thought it served them right, in a way, to be kept completely in the dark until the last minute . . .

But another part of her knew that she was being childish. She just couldn't seem to work out what to do about it.

She came home from school one day and threw her books on the kitchen table. She opened the fridge and stuck her head inside, searching for a snack that was not healthy in any way.

"Is everything okay, honey?" her mother asked. She was standing at the kitchen worktop, chopping lettuce for a salad. She gave her daughter a worried look.

"Fine." Gabriella sighed. "Don't we have anything besides fruit to eat?"

"There are carrot sticks," her mother pointed

out. Gabriella sighed even more heavily and her mother grinned. "And there's a tub of chocolate-chip ice cream in the freezer. It will probably spoil your appetite, but it sounds like you need it."

Gabriella smiled a little as she grabbed the ice cream from the freezer. "Yeah," she muttered.

"Anything I can help you with?"

Gabriella shrugged. "It's just that I never get to see Troy or Taylor any more, since they got so involved in the Battle of the Bands. They don't even have time to call me at night to talk on the phone for a little while."

Her mother put the lettuce in a bowl and started cutting up tomatoes. "I can understand why you'd feel left out."

"They don't mean to ignore me," Gabriella said loyally. "I'm sure they don't even realize what they're doing."

"Of course not," her mother agreed. "They're both nice people. But they're caught up in something very time-consuming right now. Speaking of which – how is *your* song coming along?"

"Okay," Gabriella said. She paused, then added shyly, "Pretty good, actually."

Her mother raised her eyebrows in mock surprise. "Pretty good? You must be phenomenal if you're willing to say that you're 'pretty good'!"

Gabriella laughed and blushed. "It's a great song. And Ryan even helped me with a few moves. I mean, I'm not dancing all over the place the way Sharpay does, but it's still fun."

"What do Troy and Taylor think about your number?"

There was a long silence. "Um . . ." Gabriella finally said.

Her mother raised her eyebrows again, but this time in real surprise. "Gabriella?"

"Well . . . I haven't exactly told them yet," she admitted.

"Why not? This is something you're all going through together–"

"I know, I know! But the right moment never seems to come along and anyway, they're only interested in talking about their own songs and I wasn't sure for the longest time that I would actually go through with it and–"

"–and maybe you were feeling a little left out?" her mother guessed. "So you decided to shut *them* out and keep it a secret?"

Gabriella looked glumly at her ice-cream bowl. When she heard it spelled out like that, it didn't sound so good. "Well, yeah. Maybe."

"Honey, I don't want to tell you what to do," her mother began. "But–"

"–you're going to tell me what to do," Gabriella finished with a tiny smile.

Her mother shrugged ruefully. "I'm going to *suggest* that you let your friends in on your secret. You'll feel better and I know that they would like to have the chance to support you the way you've been supporting them."

Gabriella nodded. "Yeah . . . but now that I've waited so long, it's going to be kind of awkward bringing it up, you know?"

"True. But not as awkward as having them

find out the night of the competition," her mother pointed out. "And Gabriella – I'm sure that once this is all over with, you guys will be hanging out together all the time and–" her voice took on a teasing note, "–running up the phone bill to astronomical heights, just like you used to."

Gabriella smiled at that. "I guess you're right. Thanks, Mum."

She always felt better after talking to her mother, she thought. Especially when it meant that she also got to eat chocolate-chip ice cream before dinner.

A few days later, Sharpay was walking briskly down the hall, mulling over her latest problem with her girl group and feeling a familiar sense of frustration and irritation. Charlotte just couldn't seem to stay on key, and when Alicia tried to do the hand movements that Ryan had taught them, she looked as if she were signalling a plane to come in for a landing. It wasn't good, not good at all. And Taylor – Sharpay's irritation grew even more intense when she thought about Taylor. She was . . . well, she was perfect. Which wasn't good, either. The angrier Sharpay felt, the faster she walked, until she was double-timing it down the corridor, past the gym and around the corner–

–where she almost ran into Troy and Chad.

"Whoa! Slow down, Sharpay!" Troy said, laughing. "Unless you're trying to take out the competition by mowing us down?"

"Oh, I'm sorry," Sharpay said coolly. "I hadn't noticed that there *was* any competition."

"Ouch!" Chad couldn't help but laugh at her comeback.

"You'll notice when we take the stage for Battle of the Bands," Troy promised. " 'Cause at the end of the night, Mr Matsui is going to stand on the stage and he's gonna say, 'The winner of the East High School Battle of the Bands is–' "

Too late, he remembered that they still hadn't decided on a band name.

"Yes, I heard you're having a problem naming your little band," she said sweetly. "May I suggest The Mind-Numbing Neanderthals?"

Chad frowned at that. "We have a million names!" he said hotly. "Great names! In fact, that's the only problem we have! Too many excellent ideas for names!"

She flipped her hair back and smiled haughtily. "Well, you better decide on one soon. A good name is one of the keys to impressing the judges."

"Is that right?" Troy said. "So what's your group's name?"

"For your information," she answered frostily, "it's Sharpay and the Sharpettes."

Chad rolled his eyes. "Figures," he muttered. "What was your second choice? Me, Myself and I?"

Just then, Ryan rushed up to Sharpay. "I just checked with Ms Dermot about rehearsal space," he said breathlessly. "I got four o'clock, just like you wanted."

Before she could respond, Chad greeted him with a high five. "Ryan, my man!"

"Oh, hey, Chad," Ryan responded, shooting a nervous sidelong glance at his sister.

She was looking back, her eyes narrowed suspiciously.

"Dude, your moves were awesome the other day–" Chad began.

"Um, yeah, thanks . . . er . . . dude," Ryan interrupted quickly. "Oops, gotta run, late for class. Come on, Sharpay!"

He took her arm and headed up the corridor. They moved about two feet before she shook herself free and moved in front of him, blocking his way.

"What was that all about?" she demanded. "How do you know that, that . . . *jock*? And why was he complimenting you on your moves?"

"Oh, um." Ryan thought fast. Unfortunately, his fastest thinking was . . . rather slow. "Well, that is, I'm not sure–"

However, Troy had seen the suspicious look

that Sharpay gave Ryan and he followed them along the corridor. He pretended that he had just been casually walking by when he overheard her question. Totally by accident, of course.

"Oh, Ryan was showing us some of the choreography he created for your group during English class yesterday," Troy said. "It's pretty cool."

"Oh." Sharpay looked nonplussed. On the one hand, she liked getting a compliment, even if it was from her main competitor. On the other hand, the compliment was really aimed at Ryan – and what was he *thinking*, letting other people know what they had planned before the actual night of the performance?

"Well, it's even more fabulous when you see us doing it," she said, recovering quickly. She turned to Ryan. "*Which no one will see until the actual night*. Understood?"

He gulped and nodded quickly.

The bell rang. "Good. See you later," she said, and trotted down the hall.

Ryan looked at Troy with relief. "Thanks," he said. "You really saved me."

"No problem." Troy gave him a light punch on the shoulder. "You're kind of . . . well, part of the team now. And team-mates always watch each other's backs, right? Catch you later."

He headed off for class. Ryan looked after him, stunned. *He* . . . was part of the team? He walked down the hall, dazed.

CHAPTER EIGHT

"You're doing great, Gabriella," Kelsi said. "Let's do it one more time, from the top."

"All right. But I'm not sure I'm doing that great," Gabriella said. "In fact, I think that the closer we get to the Battle of the Bands, the worse I sound!"

"That's because you're doing a number on yourself in your head," Kelsi explained. "It's one of the perils of performing. You can really psych yourself out if you're not careful."

"Great," Gabriella said glumly. "Now I don't just have to worry about my voice, I have to worry about my mind, too."

"Why don't we try that visualization technique I told you about yesterday?" Kelsi suggested.

"Okay, why not." Gabriella shrugged. "At this point, I'll try anything."

"All right. First, close your eyes and take a deep breath," Kelsi said.

Gabriella did and Kelsi began to talk in a soothing voice. "You are standing onstage. The stage is dark. You can hear people in the audience talking . . . can you visualize that?"

"Uh-huh." Only too well, Gabriella thought. Her stomach was already churning and Kelsi hadn't even got to the scary part!

"Good. Now you can hear Principal Matsui walk up to the microphone. The audience hushes. He says–" Kelsi suddenly raised her voice, "–'And now, ladies and gentlemen, Gabriella Montez, singing the sixties classic, "These Boots Are Made for Walkin'"!' And the spotlight hits you! You can feel the heat and the glare dazzles your eyes! Can you feel that?"

"Oh, yeah," Gabriella muttered. Now her palms were sweaty.

"You feel a little nervous, of course," her friend added, going back to the soothing voice of a meditation tape. "Your heart is beating quickly. Your breath is getting shallow. So you take a deep breath–" She paused while Gabriella obediently took a breath, "–and you remind yourself that you're not really nervous – you're excited! Those butterflies are the feeling of anticipation! You are filled with confidence as you remember all the hours you spent rehearsing! You are filled with strength because you know with absolute certainty that all your hard work is about to pay off! And you are filled with power because you know that you are about to give *the best performance of your life!*"

Gabriella gasped. She *did* feel strong, powerful and confident! And she *was* excited about singing!

"So you open your eyes and you sing!" Kelsi finished triumphantly.

And Gabriella did.

Four minutes later, she stared at Kelsi in wonder. Kelsi smiled smugly back.

"Wow," Gabriella said. "I really *can* sing!"

"Told you," Kelsi said.

"Hi, hi, hi!" Sharpay said brightly as she entered the choir room a few minutes after Gabriella and Kelsi had left. "Is everyone ready to put on a show?"

Taylor rolled her eyes. It's not a show, she wanted to say. This is just another *practice*. And we've practised until we're singing this stupid song in our sleep!

She sighed deeply. She used to love "Stop! In the Name of Love", she thought mournfully. Now she didn't think she'd ever be able to listen to it again.

Even Charlotte and Alicia seemed a little weary at this point.

As Ryan rushed in, Sharpay repeated herself. "I said, is everyone ready to put on a show?"

"You *bet* we are, Sharpay!" Ryan cried out, adding an extra bit of verve to his voice to make up for being late – again.

The girls just looked at him.

Oops, he thought. That may have been just a *little* bit over the top . . .

"I mean," he said more calmly, "I'm so excited to see how you guys do today. I thought the choreography was really coming together last night–"

"Yes," Sharpay interrupted. "Coming together, but not quite there. However, with a few concentrated hours of work today, I'm sure we will get to where we need to be."

"Um, Sharpay?" Alicia raised her hand hesitantly, as if asking permission to speak. Taylor barely kept herself from rolling her eyes in disgust.

"Yes, Alicia?" Sharpay inclined her head

regally and Taylor lost her inner battle. She rolled her eyes in disgust.

"The thing is, I've got, like, a major geometry test tomorrow?" Alicia said, as if she were asking a question. "And I really, really, really need to study? Because if I don't make at least a C, I'm going to flunk for the semester and my parents will kill me? So–"

"So," Sharpay interrupted briskly, "I guess you have a decision to make."

Alicia blinked, confused. "I – I do?"

"Yesss," Sharpay hissed. "Do you want to go down in history as the singer who broke up Sharpay and the Sharpettes?"

"Um, Sharpay, what history are we talking about here?" Taylor asked. It was time, she thought, to try to inject a slight note of reality into this situation.

Sharpay waved a dismissive hand. "The history that will be written when I am famous, of course! Haven't any of you watched those VH-1 specials? Every famous person always starts from humble beginnings with a small group made up of her close friends. Then one of those friends decides the demands of stardom – even *reflected* stardom – are just too much. She starts whining about too many days on the tour bus, too many bad meals backstage, too many demanding fans–"

Taylor and Charlotte exchanged confused glances. What tour bus? What backstage meals? What demanding fans?

Sharpay, honey, you are in your own little world, Taylor thought. And it sounds like a really scary place to be.

But Alicia was mesmerized as Sharpay went on.

"That friend ends up quitting the band, going back to her dumpy little hometown and then dying in obscurity – when she could have clung to the star's coat-tails and enjoyed a life of fame and glamour!" Sharpay finished with some satisfaction. Her eyes slowly swivelled in order to focus on Alicia. "Is that what you want, Alicia?

To die – alone, forgotten and poor – simply because you were afraid to fail geometry?"

"N-no," Alicia whimpered.

"Good! So let's get started!" Sharpay said briskly. "Ryan, turn on the music! Girls, line up behind me! And one, two, three, *four–*"

As the music blared from the speakers, Sharpay started singing, again giving an all-out performance, stretching her vocal cords to their limits, doing high kicks above her head, and flinging herself around the room in a frenzy of sixties-style dancing.

Taylor, Alicia and Charlotte sighed but obediently started singing the backing lyrics and moving across the room, doing the steps Ryan had taught them.

Ryan just stood on the sidelines, admiration gleaming in his eyes. The rehearsal had come so close to falling apart! It was the same old story: some people just didn't have the discipline or work ethic or sheer drive to succeed! They always wanted to take shortcuts. But Sharpay would never do that – and she'd never let anyone else do it either! She had pulled this group together in the nick of time, just as they were about to head down that long, slippery slope to the land of mediocrity.

It was times like these, he thought, when he was just so *proud* that Sharpay was his sister!

CHAPTER NINE

"Okay, how about this?" Chad asked. He held up his hands, as if framing a poster with their name on it and solemnly pronounced, "Order of the Wildcats!"

The other boys just shook their heads. "Dude," Jason said, "that makes us sound like some kind of secret society or something!"

Chad took a deep breath. He was a fount of creative ideas, an inexhaustible source of imaginative thinking, a veritable master of marketing – but he was getting just a little tired of having every single one of his band names shot down!

He took another breath, even deeper. "Fine," he said evenly. "How about Howlin' Wildcats?"

They silently shook their heads again.

"Wild Howl? The Red Hot Wildcats? Screamin' Wildcats? The Wildcat Crew?" He stopped, frustrated at the litany of 'no's. "What if it was spelled some different way? Like, um, Wyldkat Crüe?" He spelled it out for them. "And the *u* would have those two little dots over it," he explained helpfully.

They looked at him as if he were insane.

"Okay, then, *you* think of something!" he snapped, just as Troy and Ryan entered the room.

"What's going on?" Troy asked, sensing the tension.

"We still don't have a band name," Zeke shrugged.

"Oh, that," Troy said. As if he didn't have enough to worry about . . . "Well, let's start rehearsing, okay? It won't matter what our name is if we can't even stay in the same key . . ."

Half an hour later, the band was in the middle of "Twist and Shout" when Troy sensed that they were going off track. He held up his hand and said, "Okay, guys, let's stop right there—"

But the band kept playing.

"C'mon, we have to start again—"

Chad and Zeke grinned at each other as they started doing random riffs. First, Chad would strum his guitar with dramatic swinging arm movements, then Zeke would match him and add a little jump at the end for good measure. They started laughing at their own antics so much that they completely lost track of what song they were supposed to be playing.

As they kept goofing around, Troy started to get really angry. Was he the only one who cared that they were going to look like idiots in front of the whole school when they tried to play?

"Hey, enough fun and games, guys," he tried again. "We need to get serious now–"

But now Jason got into the spirit of things too, banging his drums as hard as he could and hitting the cymbals every other beat.

Troy yelled, "Stop! Stop! Stop!"

Finally the band came to a clanging halt, with just the echo of one last rim shot sounding through the auditorium.

"What's up, dude?" Chad asked. "I thought we were actually sounding pretty good there. For a few seconds at a time, at least."

Troy ran his hand through his hair in frustration. "We never end the song at the same time," he pointed out. "Zeke, you keep forgetting what key we're in. Chad, you can't keep making up lyrics whenever you feel like it! And Jason, you've gotta keep a steady beat. We're all depending on you to keep us in rhythm. C'mon, guys, the competition is in one week! We gotta get it together."

There was a brief silence as everyone stared down at the floor.

"We were just fooling around a little, Troy," Chad said.

"Yeah, this is supposed to be fun, remember?" Jason added.

"I know it's supposed to be fun!" Troy snapped. "But we also want to win, right?"

They all looked down and shuffled their feet. No one said anything.

Troy glared at them. "We do want to win," he repeated slowly. "Right?"

Finally, Chad shrugged. "Yeah, sure, Troy," he said flatly. "We're out to dominate. Go Wildcats."

Troy looked at them, frustrated and confused. Why was this so hard? And why did it feel so weird? "Okay, let's all . . . take five," he said. He walked off the stage and out of the door. *I just need to cool down a little,* he thought as he found an empty bench.

He slumped on the bench and stared into the distance. This had seemed like such a good idea a month ago. A great chance to hang out with his buddies, have some fun and then fulfil every secret rock-star fantasy by bringing a crowd of people to their feet, cheering and yelling their appreciation . . .

The only problem, he thought glumly, was that the hanging-out part was feeling more like work, the concept of fun had totally vanished after the first five minutes of rehearsal and it was becoming quite clear to him that they'd be lucky if the audience applauded politely when they had finished.

After a few moments, Troy realized that he wasn't alone. Gabriella had sat down next to him.

"Um . . . is everything okay?" she finally asked.

Troy shrugged. "I saw you standing in the back of the auditorium," he said. "What do you think?"

"Well . . . there's still a long way to go," Gabriella admitted. "But–"

"I don't know what's wrong!" Troy burst out.

"We all get along great on the basketball court! Everyone knows what he's supposed to do; we work together like a team! I thought having a band would be the same thing!"

"Except, on the basketball team, you're the captain," she pointed out gently.

He looked at her. "What's that supposed to mean?"

"Well, you're not the captain of the band," she said. "Maybe you need to back off a little."

He shook his head grimly. "The Battle of the Bands is only a week away," he said. "We can't afford to goof off. I've got to keep those guys on track, or we're going to go down in flames."

Before she could respond, Ryan came running up. "I'm sorry I'm late," he said with a gasp. "I just finished Sharpay's rehearsal! Hurry! I've got to get inside before she sees me!"

Troy sighed. "I guess I'd better get back in there," he said reluctantly.

"Can you hang out for a few more minutes?" Gabriella asked, half hoping he would say no.

But he grinned at her and said, "Believe me, I'd rather hang out with you all afternoon than go back to that train wreck of a rehearsal. I'd rather do nothing except hang out with you, as a matter of fact."

She blushed. "Oh, good. Well, I just wanted to tell you something that I guess I should have told you before, but–" she looked away and finished in a rush, "–Ms Darbus suggested that I sing a solo in the Battle of the Bands and I said yes and she signed me up and I've been rehearsing with Kelsi and I'm sorry I didn't tell you before because I guess we're kind of competing in a way even though I'm sure that I don't have a chance of winning but I was always listening to all your problems with the band plus I was feeling a little hurt because you didn't ask me to sing with you and because you never had time to hang out any more so I kept it a secret from you and I'm really sorry."

For a long moment, Troy just looked at her, his mouth hanging open. Then he grinned.

"Wow," he said. "You're singing a solo? That's great, I mean, that's really brave. I can't wait to hear you!"

"Really?"

He nodded, suddenly realizing that there had been something else missing from his life for the last month. When was the last time he had been able to sit down and really talk to Gabriella? He couldn't even remember. "And I'm sorry, too, about being so busy all the time," he added. "I guess I got a little too caught up with the band and let it kind of take over my life. I promise, when this whole thing is over, I'll make it up to you. Okay?"

"Okay." Gabriella smiled.

The doors burst open and Ryan ran out, frantic. "Troy! Come on! I only have an hour before I have to meet Sharpay to go over last-minute costume changes!" He made a little 'hurry up' motion with his hand and then ran back inside.

Troy gave a little shrug. "I gotta go," he said. "Thanks for, you know . . . listening to all my problems. Not just today, either. For the last four weeks."

"Any time," she smiled, and she meant it.

As Troy entered the auditorium through the side door, he could hear the other guys talking.

"I've just about had it with this band!" Chad complained. "I mean, come on! We're not going on tour or anything! Why do we have to work so hard?"

"Yeah, Troy acts like we're about to be signed by a big record company," Zeke agreed.

"And like he's the guy who's in charge," Jason groused.

Troy stopped, his mouth hanging open. He couldn't believe what he was hearing. These guys were supposed to be his friends! And here they were, dissing him behind his back!

But would they say all these bad things about you if they weren't really upset? a little voice in his head – the part of him that was always way too honest – whispered to him. *Maybe you should hear them out . . .*

He slipped into the shadows backstage and continued to listen.

"And *nothing* we do is ever good enough!" Zeke went on.

Troy winced. *That* was hard to hear.

But maybe, his brutally honest little voice whispered, *Zeke actually has a point? You have been riding everybody pretty hard.*

Hey, don't be so tough on yourself! Ah, at last! The other little voice, the one that always stood up for him, chimed in. *You were just worried about how the band would sound on the big night. You had their best interests at heart!*

Jason kicked his drum kit, making the cymbals jangle. "Hey, I've got a good name for this band, Chad! How about Troy Bolton and the Benchwarmers? 'Cause that's all we are, just a backdrop for Troy to be the star."

Ouch. Neither of his voices had anything to say about *that.*

Troy decided it was time to step out of the shadows. As he walked onto the stage, the others fell silent.

"Oh, um, hi, Troy," Chad said sheepishly. "I – we didn't know you were standing there."

Zeke and Jason gave each other embarrassed glances. "Yeah, listen, I didn't really mean–" Jason said.

Troy waved his hand dismissively. "No, that's okay. So, guys, I've been doing some thinking, and I think that an apology is in order–"

"Yes, I totally agree!" Ryan jumped in. "In fact, I'd say that everyone here owes Troy a huge apology!"

Troy tried to stop him. "Actually, Ryan, what I really wanted to say–"

"Don't worry, Troy, I'll handle this," Ryan said. He punched Troy in the arm. "I got your back, buddy." He turned to the rest of the band. "Is Troy being demanding? Yes! Is he forcing you to test your boundaries? Yes! Is he asking you to shoot for perfection? Yes!"

"Um, well, no . . ." Troy tried again.

But now Ryan was on a roll. "He's only being demanding because he wants the very best performance possible! If you could see how Sharpay has been running her rehearsals, you would want to work even harder! They are working day and night! And do you know why? Because you can only succeed through hard work and determination and sacrifice! That's showbiz – and that's rock 'n' roll!"

He finally came to a halt, glaring at the others, hands on hips. For a long moment, there was total silence.

Then Ryan broke the silence by saying, "So. I think *some* people need to apologize!"

Chad, Zeke and Jason looked down. Chad muttered, "Um, yeah, I guess so–"

"Actually, the only person around here who needs to apologize," Troy interrupted, "is me."

Ryan stared at him in open-mouthed shock. The other guys shuffled their feet and muttered things like, "No, that's okay, dude," and "No, worries, man." But Troy had something to say, and he wanted to say it.

"I've been taking this way too seriously and trying to run the band like–" his mind flashed to Gabriella and he smiled, "–well, like the basketball team. And I'm sorry. I mean, I know it's only rock 'n' roll–"

"But we like it!" Chad shouted. He punched Troy in the shoulder. "That's okay, Troy. We knew you just wanted us to be good. But, man–" he shook his head, "–this band stuff is harder than it looks."

Zeke and Jason nodded.

"Yeah," Zeke said. "It looks so easy on MTV."

"Maybe we just don't have the right stuff," Jason said. "Maybe we should quit."

The other boys nodded and murmured in agreement.

"I. Don't. Believe. What. I'm. Hearing."

They had totally forgotten that Ryan was still there. They turned to see him looking at them in utter shock.

"It's not that big a deal," Zeke said. "So we tried and we couldn't cut it–"

"Failure is not an option!" Ryan barked. "Did you make a basket the first time you tried?"

They all shook their heads.

"Did you dunk a ball the first time you tried?"

They shook their heads again.

Ryan was pacing back and forth. "Did you know how to . . . um . . ." He hesitated. He had come to the end of his minimal basketball knowledge and had to grope for another example. He struggled on. "You know, grab the ball after someone tries to make a basket that doesn't go in–"

"Rebound," Troy said helpfully.

"Right!" Ryan cried. "Did you know how to rebound–"

Chad's eyes brightened and he gave a howl of delight. "That's it! Ryan! Troy! You did it! We've got our name!"

The others looked at him, puzzled.

"Dudes! The band is called Rebound!"

They were all so happy, they started jumping around and high-fiving each other. Even Ryan was in the middle of the boisterous group, with Chad giving him one of his special celebratory high-five-low-fives.

In the midst of all the ruckus, they didn't notice someone standing at the back of the auditorium, staring at them in anger and shock.

Then the auditorium door slammed shut. Ryan's head whipped around.

"What was that?" he asked nervously.

"Nothing, man," Zeke said. "Hey, Ryan, come over here. Let's work some more on our band choreography . . ."

CHAPTER TEN

Gabriella had just slowly and laboriously explained the latest algebra problem to Ryan when the door to room 154 slammed open. Sharpay marched in, the light of battle in her eyes.

"How could you?" she yelled at Ryan.

He jumped up and scurried back a few paces. "How could I what?"

"How could you help Troy Bolton with his band?" she yelled, even louder.

Gabriella stood up and tried to intervene. "Sharpay, there's no reason to get upset," she said reasonably. "Yes, Ryan has been doing choreography for both of you, but your bands are so different! It's not as if you guys will be using the same moves–"

"I don't care!" Sharpay was screeching now. "You are my brother and you are supposed to be working for me and nobody but me!"

Ryan stiffened at that. "I'm not your slave! I have talent of my own, you know and it just so happens that someone else recognized it! And *you* were the one who put together an all-girl group in the first place, so I couldn't even be onstage!"

Sharpay gasped. Ryan had never *dared* to argue with her before! What was going on here? Her universe was spinning out of control! She opened her mouth to yell something else – she wasn't sure quite what, but it was going to be *scathing* – and then looked even more shocked.

No sound was coming out of her mouth.

She tried again, holding her throat.

"Ah, ah, ah," she said.

"Sharpay? Are you all right?" Gabriella was staring at her, concerned.

Ryan just looked scared. "She's lost her voice," he said in a hushed tone. "And just one day before the Battle of the Bands, too!"

Alicia was crying.

Charlotte looked pale with despair.

Ryan was the picture of distress.

Taylor shrugged nonchalantly. "Oh, well," she said. "There goes our chance to go down in history as the founding members of Sharpay and the Sharpettes."

Sharpay gave a little whimper. She was seated, her head in her hands, as the others hovered around her, unsure of what to do. Ryan and Gabriella had helped her to the choir room and explained the situation to Alicia, Charlotte and Taylor. Now they all stood around, staring at each other.

"We'll have to withdraw from the competition," Alicia said.

Another whimper from Sharpay.

"And my dad was going to bring his golfing partner!" Charlotte cried. "He works for a record label!"

The whimper became a moan.

"Maybe you could try lip-synching?" Ryan suggested feebly.

His sister raised her head long enough to give him a withering look.

"Sorry," he muttered. "I panicked."

Taylor sighed impatiently. "This isn't grand opera, people! There's a very simple solution standing right here in front of us!" She pointed to Gabriella. "This girl is a great singer! I can teach her the song and moves tonight and she can join the group."

She hesitated, then said to Gabriella, "That is, if you'd be willing to do that. I'm sorry, I know we've all been kind of busy with the Battle of the Bands – well, what I really mean is that *I've* been too busy to spend time with you. And now I'm asking for a really, really big favour. But if you'd consider it . . ."

Gabriella smiled. "Thanks so much, Taylor. It means a lot that you'd ask me. But–" she hesitated, then took the plunge, "–the thing is – and I'm really sorry I didn't tell you earlier – but I kind of worked up a little number on my own. A solo."

"Ah . . ." Sharpay's attempt at a scream came out as little more than a gasp. She mouthed the words, "a *solo*?" in shock.

"Really?" Taylor beamed at her friend. "That's awesome! What song did you pick?"

"These Boots Are Made for Walkin," Gabriella said, relieved at Taylor's reaction. "It's this cool song from the sixties–"

"First sung by Nancy Sinatra, it went to number one in February 1966, a month after its release," Taylor said. "Great choice."

Sharpay gaped at them. They were completely ignoring the major crisis that had befallen *her*!

And her group, of course. She waved her hands in the air to signal that their attention needed to be refocused. On her. Right now.

Ryan saw the wave and loyally jumped in. "What are we going to do about Sharpay's performance?"

"There's a very simple solution," Gabriella pointed out. "Taylor, you know this song backwards and forwards and you have a fabulous voice—"

"Yes!" Charlotte squealed. "Taylor, you should take Sharpay's part!"

"That would be perfect!" Alicia agreed.

They clapped their hands with glee. Then Sharpay started whimpering again. They all turned to look at her and Sharpay saw the truth in their eyes. They had actually forgotten she was there!

A tear rolled slowly down her cheek.

Taylor put her arm around Sharpay's shoulders. "Now, don't cry," she said. "After all, the name of the group is Sharpay and the

Sharpettes, isn't it? We can't go on without you! We just have to figure something else out . . ."

The auditorium was packed with people on the night of the Battle of the Bands. In fact, it was standing room only.

Gabriella stood backstage, peeking through the curtains at the crowd and listening to the excited buzz that filled the room. She gulped. Even after performing the lead role in *Twinkle Towne*, she wasn't totally confident in the spotlight. Actually, she felt as if she was about to faint from stage fright. The only good thing, she thought, is that I'm just singing a solo. Everyone wants to hear the bands rockin' out; nobody will care about my little song. So, no big deal, right?

She closed her eyes and leaned her head against the wall. No. It still felt like a really big deal.

"Hey, Gabriella!"

She heard Troy's whisper behind her and opened her eyes again, smiling.

"Hi, Troy!" She was so happy to see him! All

the memories of performing together in the musical flooded through her mind. Singing onstage wasn't torture, she reminded herself. It was actually really fun! "How are you?"

He nodded. "Okay." He caught the look in her eye and grinned. "Yeah, I'm a little nervous, too. Goes with the territory, right?"

They both laughed softly, showbiz veterans at 16.

"Listen, I just came by to say good luck tonight. I mean–" he hastily corrected himself, remembering one of the many lectures on theatrical tradition given by Ms Darbus, "–break a leg. I'm sure you'll be great."

"Good luck to you, too." She smiled. "I can't wait to see Chad do the twist."

"Yeah, it should be a showstopper," he said dryly and they both laughed again.

At that moment, Chad's head poked out from the other side of the curtain. "C'mon, Troy," he called. "We gotta get our equipment set up."

"Okay," Troy said. He turned back to

Gabriella. "So . . . tomorrow night? Dinner and a movie? No cancellations allowed?"

"That sounds wonderful."

"Good. See you later." He grinned and dashed off.

Principal Matsui stood in front of the microphone at centre stage and cleared his throat. The sound echoed through the room, silencing the energized chatter of the audience.

"Ladies and gentlemen, welcome to East High's first annual Battle of the Bands!" he cried. "I want to thank every student who has worked so hard to bring you all a rockin' good time tonight!" He paused, gratified as the audience's excitement finally translated into the wild applause he had been waiting to hear for so many long, silent months of giving assembly announcements. "First up, we have Troy Bolton, Chad Danforth, Zeke Baylor and Jason Cross, playing 'Twist and Shout'. Ladies and gentlemen, I present to you . . . Rebound!"

The audience cheered wildly as the curtain rose, revealing the boys standing with their instruments under blue stage lights.

"And one! Two! One, two, three, four!" Troy called out.

They swung into the song, fast and furious. Jason was driving the beat with his wild drumming, Zeke was keeping up with a rapid bass beat, and Troy and Chad matched each other, riff for riff, on the guitar.

Troy started singing the lyrics first, leaping around the stage and striking his very best rock-star poses. Within a few bars, the audience members were dancing and singing along.

Backstage, Ryan watched, his eyes gleaming as all his hard work came to fruition. He was so caught up in the pounding rhythm that he even found himself doing a little dance himself, right next to the wooden tree cutouts.

After the first chorus, Troy backed off and nodded to Chad. Chad nodded back, grinning, and took centre stage. He sang the second verse, adding a few spontaneous Wildcat howls, and then did the twist . . . perfectly. The audience went wild and the boys of Rebound grinned their congratulations.

By the end of the song, Zeke had performed a quick bass solo and Jason had brought the house down with his special drumstick-twirling technique. The band ended with one loud, triumphant chord, then bowed quickly as the curtain fell.

In the wings, Taylor, Alicia, Charlotte and Gabriella whispered congratulations as the boys ran off the stage. Sharpay even thawed enough to give Zeke a little wave, which made him grin.

Next, it was Gabriella's turn. She walked onstage, wearing a colourful print minidress and go-go boots. Her hair was done in a sixties-style pageboy with a flip at the ends. She felt totally unlike herself – which was actually a good thing in her opinion. Her knees were shaking and her hands were trembling. It helped to imagine that she was someone else entirely. The spotlight came on and she blinked. From the corner of her eye, she saw Kelsi give her an encouraging nod as she flipped a switch and the music began playing.

Gabriella started to sing. After the first few notes, she forgot that she was onstage and in the spotlight. She was totally into the song, belting it out with sass and spirit. As she started doing the simple choreography Ryan had designed for her, she could hear some people in the audience yell and whistle.

She dared to sneak a quick peek at the crowd. People were on their feet! They were clapping along! They were smiling! Even Ms Darbus was doing a little shimmy-shake, right there in the front row. She caught Gabriella's eye and gave her a big thumbs-up.

Gabriella broke out into a huge smile. *Now* she remembered why singing in front of a crowd was so much fun! In fact, she couldn't believe she had ever been scared of it!

When she finished, she bowed and ran off the stage, breathless with excitement.

"You go, girl!" Taylor cried. "That was excellent!"

"Thanks!" Gabriella grinned. She glanced further backstage and saw Troy standing alone. He smiled and gave her a wave of congratulation, but before he could speak, Principal Matsui called out, "And now, ladies and gentlemen, Sharpay and the Sharpettes!"

"Break a leg," Gabriella whispered as Taylor, Sharpay, Alicia and Charlotte ran onstage. The four girls stood in the spots they had become so accustomed to over the weeks of rehearsal. As the curtain rose, Ryan flipped the switch of the sound system and the music for "Stop! In the Name of Love" blared from the speakers.

Taylor sang her heart out, her voice ringing through the auditorium with power, confidence and soul. In the audience, the choir teacher Mrs Jones smiled with pride.

Alicia and Charlotte were pitch-perfect as they hummed and doo-wopped away in the background. Sharpay stood next to them, swaying to the music and mouthing the words.

Then, right after the second verse, Taylor stopped singing and moved back to stand with the backing singers. As the music continued its pounding, upbeat tempo, Sharpay stepped forward and began performing the dance that she had planned on doing from the very beginning.

She shimmied. She gyrated. She did high kicks. She whirled across the stage and then whirled back again . . .

She didn't think it was possible for the audience to scream any louder, but it was. And they were screaming for her!

Sharpay smiled giddily. Maybe she had lost her voice, maybe she couldn't wow them with her singing, but she was right where she always knew she was destined to be – in the spotlight!

When the last group had performed, Principal Matsui told the audience that there would be a 15-minute break as the judges' scores were tallied. Gabriella, the members of Rebound and Sharpay and the Sharpettes spent those 15 minutes backstage, excitedly congratulating each other over and over again for their great performances.

Finally, the Principal called all the groups back onstage. He held up an envelope.

"The judges had a very difficult time selecting a winner," he said. "All of the bands performed extraordinarily well. But they finally did choose someone to award the first Battle of the Bands trophy to. And the winner – based not just on talent, not just on hard work, but on incredible dedication in the face of adversity – is Sharpay Evans!"

Sharpay's hands flew to her face in complete surprise – well, almost. It was never really a *complete* surprise when she won, after all.

She rushed forward to take the trophy from Principal Matsui, then grabbed the microphone to address the crowd. She wanted to say what an *honour* this was, how she never *expected* it, and just *how much* all the little people behind the scenes had helped her . . . then she remembered: she couldn't talk.

She frowned slightly, then shrugged and settled for a smile and a heartfelt wave for the audience instead.

As Alicia and Charlotte rushed forward to hug her, Gabriella murmured to Taylor, "I wonder how long it will be before Sharpay gets her voice back?"

"Not long enough," Taylor said with feeling, and they both laughed.

At that moment, Troy walked past Sharpay. "Congratulations, you really deserved that trophy!" he said. Then he approached Gabriella and Taylor. "Hey, Taylor! Congrats on winning the Battle of the Bands."

"Oh, we didn't win," Taylor said quickly. "Sharpay did."

"I think your singing might have had just a little bit to do with that," Troy said, teasing. "I never knew you had such a great voice!"

"Well . . ." She shrugged modestly.

"Yeah, Taylor, you were awesome!" Chad had now joined the group, still bouncing up and down with excitement. "You too, Gabriella! And you've got some cool moves!"

"Well, that's all thanks to Ryan. Anyway, it's too bad you guys couldn't have won, too," Gabriella said. "After all your hard work . . . Rebound sounded great!"

"Winning's not the important thing," Troy said. "The best part of forming Rebound was having a chance to hang with my boys."

"You got that right, bro!" Chad declared.

Zeke and Jason ran up. "Hey, you guys, we're all going out for pizza! Do you want to come?"

Everyone nodded eagerly. As they were heading out of the side door, Gabriella caught sight of Ryan.

"Hey, Ryan, you've gotta come hang out with us!" she called.

Ryan looked shy, nervous and hopeful, all at once. "Really?"

"Yeah, of course!" Troy said. "If it weren't for you, none of this would have happened."

"I'd still be standing like a statue when I played," Zeke said.

"I never would have learned to twirl my drumsticks," Jason pointed out.

"And I'd still fall over every time I tried to do the twist," Chad added earnestly.

"Well, okay . . ." He looked at Gabriella. "As long as I don't have to figure out the exact circumference of the pizza . . ."

She grinned. "Consider this a night off from algebra, Ryan! And enjoy it!"

Laughing, they all went out of the building into the night.

Something new is on the way!

Look for the next book in the High School Musical: Stories from East High series . . .

WILDCAT SPIRIT

By Catherine Hapka

Based on the Disney Channel Original Movie *High School Musical*, written by Peter Barsocchini

"Go Wildcats!" Troy Bolton shouted as the basketball left his fingertips. A second later it swished through the basket – nothing but net.

He grinned as his team-mates cheered. Troy's best friend, Chad Danforth, raced in and grabbed the ball, then sprang up and dunked it.

"That's what I'm talkin' about!" Chad crowed, doing a little victory dance under the basket.

Meanwhile, a couple of other team-mates,

Zeke Baylor and Jason Cross, jogged over to give Troy a high five. "We are so ready for the game next Saturday," Zeke said. "We're going to totally slay Central!"

A whistle blew, echoing through the gym. "That's enough for today, guys." Coach Bolton, who was also Troy's father, surveyed his team proudly. "Have a great weekend and don't forget that East High's Spirit Week starts on Monday. I expect you guys to lead the way. Nobody has more school spirit than this Wildcats team!" His serious face cracked into a smile as the team cheered. Then he winked. "I also expect to see one of you guys up there reigning as Spirit King at the big dance on Saturday night."

"Gee, I wonder who's going to win that title?" Chad said loudly, putting one finger to his chin and pretending to think hard.

The rest of the guys laughed. Zeke started the chant and the others picked up on it – "Troy! Troy! *Troy!* TROYTROYTROY!" Chad pumped his fist in the air as he shouted along.

Coach Bolton grinned and strode off towards his office. Troy gave Chad a shove, making him drop the basketball that was tucked under his arm.

"Quit it, bro," Troy said. "If anybody should win that Spirit King title, it's Jason. He's the one who sank that three-pointer that won us the game last week."

"Nice try, Mr Modesty." Chad scurried after the ball, which was bouncing across the floor.

"Yeah, give it up, Troy," Jason said. "Who could possibly have more school spirit than our superstar team captain? Everyone knows that title is yours – the only question is who's going to be your queen."

Zeke nodded. "Dude, you could show up wearing a hat on Pyjamas Day and pyjamas on School Colours Day and you'd still win it in a walk. Nobody can touch you, man!"

"Dad always told me, don't count your baskets until the points are on the board," Troy said, glancing off in the direction in which his father had just gone. "So I'm not counting on anything."

"My man Troy does have a point," Jason said. "Don't forget, the teachers are the ones who make the decision. And who knows how they think? They could decide to give the title to one of their pet science nerds or something."

"No way!" Zeke shuddered, looking horrified. "A science nerd as Spirit King? That's just wrong."

"Yeah," one of the other guys muttered. "But it's possible."

"Whatever." Chad dribbled and shot, sending the basketball bouncing off the rim. "I just remembered, I need to hit the mall this weekend and buy some new PJs. My mum said if I leave the house in any of mine, she'll disown me and go into the Witness Protection Programme."

Troy laughed. He'd seen Chad's wardrobe, and he couldn't blame his mum. Every pair of pyjamas Chad owned had huge holes in the knees; he was sometimes a little *too* enthusiastic when he played sock basketball in his room. The guy was obsessed. But that was one of the reasons Troy liked him – he was obsessed with basketball, too.

"I still can't believe they want us to wear our pyjamas to school," Jason commented as the team wandered toward the locker room.

"Yeah, but think about how comfortable we'll be," one of the other guys said.

"I just hope I can stay awake during physics," said Zeke.

As the guys continued to discuss the pros and cons of Pyjamas Day, Troy was thinking about something else. He leaned back against the wall. "Maybe I need to hit the mall, too," he said, mostly to himself. "I want to get something cool to wear next Saturday night."

Chad sidled up to him, dribbling from hand to hand between his legs. "Sounds like someone's already thinking about the Spirit Ball," he said with a smirk. "So when are you going to ask her?"

Troy could feel his cheeks going as red as his Wildcats gym shorts. "I don't know what you're talking about," he mumbled.

But he knew *exactly* what Chad was talking about – Gabriella Montez. Ever since Troy had met Gabriella, she seemed to be all he could think about. She was intelligent, gorgeous, funny and sweet. He'd never met a girl like her. Even the thought of going to a school dance with her on his arm, swaying together to the music, made him shiver. All he had to do was work out the perfect way to ask her . . .

". . . so he can't ask her," Jason was saying.

"Huh?" Troy blinked, his fantasies dissolving instantly. "What did you just say?"

"Yo, Jason's right," Zeke put in, reaching out and stealing the ball from Chad. "You can't ask her, dude. It's a Sadie Hawkins dance."

"A whosie whatsit?" Chad asked, wrinkling his nose.

"Sadie Hawkins," Zeke explained. He bounced the ball against the wall in time with his words. "That means the girls have to ask the guys, not the other way around."

Disney

HIGH SCHOOL MUSICAL

STORIES FROM EAST HIGH #2

WILDCAT SPIRIT

By Catherine Hapka

Based on the Disney Channel Original Movie *High School Musical*, written by Peter Barsocchini

Parragon

Bath New York Singapore Hong Kong Cologne Delhi Melbourne

First published by Parragon in 2007
Parragon
Queen Street House
4 Queen Street
Bath BA1 1HE, UK

ISBN 978-1-4075-0343-1

Printed in China

CHAPTER ONE

"Go, Wildcats!" Troy Bolton shouted as the basketball left his fingertips. A second later it swished through the basket – nothing but net.

He grinned as his team-mates cheered. Troy's best friend, Chad Danforth, raced in and grabbed the ball, then sprang up and dunked it.

"That's what I'm talkin' about!" Chad crowed, doing a little victory dance under the basket.

Meanwhile, a couple of other team-mates,

Zeke Baylor and Jason Cross, jogged over to give Troy a high five.

"We are so ready for the game next Saturday," Zeke said. "We're going to totally slay Central!"

A whistle blew, echoing through the gym. "That's enough for today, guys." Coach Bolton, who was also Troy's father, surveyed his team proudly. "Have a great weekend and don't forget that East High's Spirit Week starts on Monday. I expect you guys to lead the way. Nobody has more school spirit than this Wildcats team!" His serious face cracked into a smile as the team cheered, and he winked. "I also expect to see one of you guys up there reigning as Spirit King at the big dance on Saturday night."

"Gee, I wonder who's going to win that title?" Chad said loudly, putting one finger to his chin and pretending to think hard.

The rest of the guys laughed. Zeke started the chant, and the others picked up on it – "Troy! Troy! *Troy*! TROYTROYTROY!" Chad pumped his fist in the air as he shouted along.

Coach Bolton grinned and strode off towards his office. Troy gave Chad a shove, making him drop the basketball tucked under his arm.

"Quit it, bro," Troy said. "If anybody should win that Spirit King title, it's Jason. He's the one who sank the three-pointer that won us the game last week."

"Nice try, Mr Modesty." Chad scurried after the ball, which was bouncing across the floor.

"Yeah, give it up, Troy," Jason said. "Who could possibly have more school spirit than our superstar team captain? Everyone knows that title is yours – the only question is who's going to be your queen."

Zeke nodded. "Dude, you could show up wearing a hat on Pyjamas Day and pyjamas on School Colours Day and you'd still win it in a walk. Nobody can touch you, man!"

"Dad always tells me, don't count your baskets until the points are on the board," Troy said, glancing in the direction in which his father had just gone. "So I'm not counting on anything."

"My man Troy does have a point," Jason said. "Don't forget, the teachers are the ones who make the decision. And who knows how they think? They could decide to give the title to one of their pet science nerds or something."

"No way!" Zeke shuddered, looking horrified. "A science nerd as Spirit King? That's just wrong."

"Yeah," one of the other guys muttered. "But it's possible."

"Whatever." Chad dribbled and shot, sending the basketball bouncing off the rim. "I just remembered, I need to hit the mall this weekend and buy some new PJs. My mum said if I leave the house in any of mine, she'll disown me and go into the Witness Protection Programme."

Troy laughed. He'd seen Chad's wardrobe, and he couldn't blame his mum. Every pair of pyjamas Chad owned had huge holes in the knees; he was sometimes a little *too* enthusiastic when he played sock basketball in his room. The guy was obsessed. But that was one of the reasons Troy liked him – he was obsessed with basketball, too.

"I still can't believe they want us to wear our pyjamas to school," Jason commented as the team headed towards the locker room.

"Yeah, but think about how comfortable we'll be," one of the other guys said.

"I just hope I can stay awake during physics class," said Zeke.

As the guys continued to discuss the pros and cons of wearing pyjamas to school, Troy was thinking about something else. He leaned back against the wall.

"Maybe I need to hit the mall, too," he said, mostly to himself. "I want to get something cool to wear next Saturday night."

Chad sidled up to him, dribbling from hand to hand between his legs.

"Sounds like someone's already thinking about the Spirit Ball," he said with a smirk. "So when are you going to ask her?"

Troy could feel his cheeks going as red as his

Wildcats gym shorts. "I don't know what you're talking about," he mumbled.

But he knew *exactly* what Chad was talking about – Gabriella Montez. Ever since Troy had met Gabriella, she seemed to be all he could think about. She was smart, gorgeous, funny and sweet. He'd never met a girl like her. Even the thought of going to a school dance with her on his arm, swaying to the music and holding her close, made him shiver. All he had to do now was figure out the perfect way to ask her. But what could that be?

". . . so he can't ask her," Jason was saying.

"Huh?" Troy blinked, his fantasies dissolving instantly. "What did you just say?"

"Yo, Jason's right," Zeke put in, reaching out and stealing the ball from Chad. "You can't ask her, dude. It's a Sadie Hawkins dance."

"A whosie whatzit?" Chad asked, wrinkling his nose.

"Sadie Hawkins," Zeke explained. He bounced the ball against the wall in time with his words. "That means the girls have to ask the guys, not the other way around."

Now that he mentioned it, Troy remembered hearing something about that at the last school assembly. Somehow, it hadn't really sunk in until right now. "Oh, right," he murmured.

Chad was scratching his head through his mop of curly hair. "Who the heck is this Sadie Hawkins and why is she messing with our dance?"

"I don't know," Jason told him. "But it means you won't be able to beg every girl in school to go with you, Danforth."

One of the other guys laughed. "Uh-oh, looks like Chad'll be going stag!"

"No way," Chad exclaimed. "The ladies will be beating down my door. I'll just have to decide which one to grace with my studly presence."

Troy smiled as the rest of the team continued giving Chad a hard time. *So what if it's a Sadie Hawkins dance?* he asked himself. *No big deal. Actually, it makes my life easier. All I have* to do is sit back and wait for an invite from Gabriella . . .

* * *

At that very moment, Gabriella was gathering up her things after the latest Scholastic Decathlon meeting. "See you all next week," she said with a smile. "Don't forget your school spirit!"

One of the other girls groaned. "I almost forgot," she said. "It'll be a whole week of rah-rah type sports stuff . . ."

". . . and silly pep rallies and dressing up like dorks . . ." said Martha, another team member.

". . . and the basketball team acting like Neanderthals," finished a skinny boy with glasses, named Timothy. "Even more than usual, I mean."

"Come on, it could be fun!" Gabriella said, laughing at their sour faces.

Her best friend, Taylor, pursed her lips. "Easy for you to say," she said. "You're just looking forward to going to that Spirit Ball next weekend with Troy."

Gabriella blushed. "That's not the only reason," she protested. "I think the whole thing will be fun. I've never been part of a school Spirit Week before."

"Really?" Martha looked surprised.

"Really." Gabriella felt a twinge of sadness as she thought about all the schools she'd attended in her life. And thanks to her mother's job, she'd attended a *lot* of them before ending up at East High at the beginning of the winter semester.

But that's all over now, she reminded herself. *Mum promised we won't move again until after I graduate.*

The others were moving towards the classroom door, still discussing Spirit Week. Gabriella grabbed her bag and hurried to join them.

"Want to go shopping on Sunday?" she asked Taylor. "I want to look for something to wear to the dance."

"Sure." Taylor smiled. "But don't worry – Troy will think you look gorgeous no matter what you wear."

The others overheard. "So when are you going to ask him, Gabriella?" Martha asked eagerly.

"Ask him?" Gabriella echoed. "What do you mean? Call me a traditionalist, but I was sort of hoping *he* would be the one to ask *me* . . . "

Taylor shook her head. "Not this time," she said. "Sadie Hawkins dance, remember?"

"Really? Are you sure?" Gabriella stopped short in the doorway and turned to stare at her friend. "I don't remember hearing that."

"That's because you were too busy giggling at everything Troy said during the last assembly," Taylor said. "Principal Matsui mentioned the Sadie Hawkins thing at least three times."

"Oh." Gabriella gulped, staring out into the hallway. She'd never asked a boy out before. "Um, okay. I guess I have to ask him, then. Better to get it over with as soon as poss–" She let her voice trail off as she spotted Sharpay Evans walking by with her brother, Ryan. Or, more accurately, *flouncing* by. Sharpay never did anything as ordinary as *walking.*

"Hello, girls and boys," Sharpay said, striking a dramatic pose as she leaned against a pillar. "Talking about the Spirit Ball?"

"That's what it sounded like to me," Ryan spoke up, nodding at what his sister had just said. He might have helped the other kids during the Battle of the Bands, but his true loyalty was still with Sharpay. Basically, if she said, "Jump" he'd ask, "How high?"

Not bothering to wait for anyone else to say anything, Sharpay stared down her nose at Gabriella. "Do my little ears deceive me, or did I just hear you say you're planning to ask Troy to be your date?"

"Of course she is," Taylor said. "Who else would she ask?"

Sharpay completely ignored Taylor. Her eyes were trained on Gabriella's face like a pair of charcoal-lined, mascara-coated laser beams. Gabriella stared back, feeling vaguely nervous. Sharpay and Ryan had been the stars of every school musical except the last one – Gabriella and Troy had beaten them to the lead roles that time. Gabriella was pretty sure Sharpay still hadn't quite forgotten that – or forgiven them for it.

"Well, if you want *my* advice . . ." Sharpay began.

"Um, actually, I don't remember hearing her ask for it," Taylor said.

Once again, Sharpay ignored her. "If you want my advice, you'll play it cool," she told Gabriella.

Ryan nodded wisely. "Sound advice."

"Play it cool? What do you mean?" Gabriella asked.

Sharpay shrugged, tossing her blonde hair behind her shoulder with a practised flick of her chin.

"This is Troy Bolton we're talking about here," she said.

Yeah, Gabriella thought. Thanks for the news bulletin.

But Sharpay wasn't finished. "If you want a boy like Troy to take you seriously, you'd better not look too eager. *If* you know what I mean."

Gabriella wasn't entirely sure she did. But at that moment, she heard her mobile phone ring inside her bag.

"Excuse me," she said, wondering if it was Troy calling. He should be getting out of basketball practice around now . . .

"Hello?" she said into the phone.

Her mother's voice answered, sounding tired and distracted. "Hey, sweetie, it's me. It looks like I'm going to be late for dinner tonight."

"Again?" Gabriella said with a sigh. "That's the third time this week! Doesn't your company know you have a life?"

"Sorry. No lives allowed." Her mother laughed, but she still sounded distracted. "See you later, okay?"

Gabriella said goodbye and hung up.

"Everything okay?" Taylor asked her.

"Just Mum working too hard again. But what else is new?" Gabriella shrugged.

Taylor laughed. "Overachieving runs in the

family, huh?"

Just then there was a shrill shriek of laughter from Sharpay.

"What's so funny?" Gabriella asked, tucking her phone back into her bag.

"Your little brainiac friends here just asked who I thought would win Spirit King and Queen," Sharpay replied. She patted her hair. "Stupid question from such a smart bunch, don't you think? I would have thought that the queen, at least, was obvious. Toodles, children!"

She started off down the hall with Ryan hurrying along at her heels. Then she paused and glanced back over her shoulder.

"Remember what I said, Gabriella," she added. "You don't want to look too eager, am I right?"

"Sure," Gabriella said. Sometimes it was easier just to follow Ryan's lead and agree with whatever Sharpay said.

CHAPTER TWO

"Check it out." Chad elbowed Troy in the ribs. "There's your girlfriend."

Troy looked where Chad was staring. Sure enough, Gabriella was sitting across the mall food court with Taylor and Martha and a few other friends.

"Come on," Troy said. "Let's go say hi."

He called to Zeke and Jason, who were browsing the sale racks in front of the nearby CD shop. As the four of them made their way across the crowded food court, Troy couldn't take his eyes off Gabriella, who was sipping a drink and listening to the other girls talk.

Too bad we missed each other after practice on Friday, Troy thought. *And then she was away at her Scholastic-competition thingy all day yesterday. But this is the perfect chance for her to ask me to the dance.*

Gabriella spotted Troy when he was still a few tables away. Seeing him always made her smile and today was no exception. He looked amazing in his Wildcats team jacket and faded jeans.

"Look," she said. "Here come the guys."

"Perfect." Taylor sat up a little straighter. "I was planning to ask Chad to the dance on Monday. But I might as well do it now and be ahead of schedule."

Gabriella ducked her head to hide a smile. Taylor was a very practical person. It shouldn't be a surprise that she would treat asking a boy for a date like . . . well, like some kind of chemistry equation to be solved as quickly as possible.

Soon the boys reached the table.

"Hey, wassup?" Chad said, reaching for one of Taylor's chips without bothering to ask.

"Hi," Troy added, with a warm smile just for Gabriella.

She smiled back. "Hi," she said.

Meanwhile Taylor pointed one finger at Chad. "I'm glad you're here," she said briskly. "Chad, will you be my date for the Spirit Ball next Saturday?"

Jason and Zeke immediately started whooping and whistling. "Whoa, check out the ladies' man!" Jason crowed, slapping Chad on the back so hard that he almost pushed him into the plate of chips.

"Yeah," Zeke added. "Guess you weren't just fronting when you said the girls would be falling at your feet. Who knew you'd be the first guy on the team with a date?"

Chad's cheeks were turning red. "Uh, um . . ."

Gabriella traded an amused smile with Troy. It wasn't often that Chad Danforth was rendered speechless!

"Well?" Taylor said, sounding impatient.

Chad shrugged as his buddies continued to hoot and holler. "Thanks for the offer, babe," he said with a goofy grin. "I'll check my book and get back to you, okay?"

Taylor frowned. "What's that supposed to mean?" she demanded. "Will you go with me, or not?"

Chad held up both hands in front of him. "Whoa, what's with the pressure?" he exclaimed. "I just told you I'd let you know."

"Yeah, chill out," Jason said. "He has to make sure he doesn't already have a date with a supermodel that night."

Zeke had just swiped one of Taylor's chips. He laughed so hard that it almost flew out of his mouth. "Good one, bro!" he said, trading a high five with Jason.

"Shut up, dude." Chad punched him on the arm. "You're not helping."

As the other three guys shoved one another

around, Troy slid into the empty chair beside Gabriella. "So – speaking of the big dance . . . it should be fun, huh?" he said.

"Yeah. Fun." Gabriella barely heard him. She was too busy fuming over Chad's behaviour towards Taylor. How could he act like such a jerk? Everyone knew that he and Taylor liked each other. Although at the moment she wasn't sure what Taylor saw in him . . .

Troy cleared his throat and leaned a little closer. "It's pretty cool how they made it a Susie Hawkins dance, isn't it?"

"It's *Sadie* Hawkins," Gabriella corrected automatically. But once again, she wasn't really paying full attention to Troy. She was sure that Taylor was feeling hurt by the way Chad was acting. And Chad was so busy clowning around with Zeke and Jason that he didn't even seem to notice.

Why are guys such jerks sometimes? Gabriella wondered. *It's like they don't even notice that other people have feelings.*

"So anyway . . ." Troy began.

Gabriella never even got the chance to hear what Troy was about to say. At that moment, Taylor stood up and stormed off.

"Taylor, wait!" Gabriella cried. Leaving her drink on the table, she raced after her friend.

Fifteen minutes later, Troy was still thinking about Gabriella. Why hadn't she asked him to the dance? He'd certainly given her enough of an opening.

He wandered through the mall with the other guys, but he wasn't paying attention to the shop they were passing. When they reached their favourite sports shop, Jason had to ask Troy three times if he wanted to go inside.

"Sorry," Troy said, shaking his head to clear it of all thoughts of Gabriella. "Guess I'm a little out of it."

"Thinking about the big game next weekend?" Zeke asked.

"Nah, he's probably deciding which pyjamas to wear to school tomorrow," Jason guessed.

Chad rolled his eyes. "Get a clue, dorks," he said. "He's thinking about what he's always thinking about these days. I'll give you a hint – her initials are GM. And I'm *not* talking about the car company."

"You caught me this time," Troy admitted with a rueful smile. "It just doesn't make sense. Taylor asked you. Why didn't Gabriella ask me?"

Chad shrugged and poked at a pair of baseball boots on the sale rack outside the sports shop. "Why do girls do anything, man?" he said. "Maybe she found another guy or something."

"Yeah, right." Troy knew that wasn't the problem. He just didn't know what the problem *was*. "Come on," he said, deciding not to think about it. "Let's go inside."

"Troy! Hey, Troy!"

Hearing his name as he entered the shop, Troy turned to look. So did his friends.

"Yo, cheerleader alert," Jason said.

Sure enough, several members of East High's cheerleading squad were rushing towards them from the back of the shop. In the lead was a perky, curly-haired cheerleader named Ami. She was waving and calling Troy's name.

"Hey, Ami," he greeted her when she reached him. "What's up?"

"I'm soooo glad I ran into you, Troy!" she cried, brushing a springy lock of hair out of her face. "Will you go to the dance with me?"

Troy was startled by the invitation. Somehow, it hadn't even occurred to him that anyone other than Gabriella would ask him. Didn't the whole school know by now that they were an item?

But Ami was gazing at him with a bright smile, waiting for an answer. "Um – uh – I'm sorry," he stammered, trying to ignore his friends, who were snorting and nudging each other as they watched. "I – I think I'm going with somebody else."

"Oh." Ami looked disappointed, but then she shrugged and turned to Jason with a smile. "How about you? Want to go with me?"

"Sure!" Jason said immediately. "I'm so there!"

"Cool!" Ami patted him on the arm. "It's a date. See you at school tomorrow. I can't wait to see all you guys in your jammies!" She turned and hurried off with her friends, giggling.

Jason stared after her with a goofy look on his face. He touched the spot on his arm where she'd patted him. "Whoa," he said. "Sorry to swoop in like that, Troy. But you blew it, bro. She's totally hot!"

"Guess I did. Your gain, man." Troy shrugged and smiled. Sure, half the guys in school would kill to go to the dance with a girl like Ami. But not him. He was holding out for one very special girl.

Gabriella was lost in thought as she wandered up the front walkway of her house. She'd managed to convince Taylor that Chad was just kidding around in front of his basketball buddies. Of course he would say yes. Finally, Taylor had agreed to give him another chance to act like a human being and accept her invitation. Gabriella was relieved. But the whole incident had left a funny taste in her mouth.

I know Chad likes Taylor, she thought. So why would he act that way when she asked him out? It just doesn't make sense.

She chewed on her lower lip as she reached for the front door. A thought had just occurred to her. A very scary, weird thought: could Sharpay actually know what she was talking about?

"No way," Gabriella whispered.

She entered the front hallway and slung her shopping bags onto a chair. She could hear her mother's voice drifting towards her from the direction of the kitchen. It sounded as if she was on the phone.

Gabriella headed down the hall. As she got closer, she realized her mother was using her business voice. She frowned. Could she really be taking a business call on Sunday afternoon?

She pushed open the kitchen door. Her mother was standing with her back to Gabriella, staring out of the window over the sink as she talked.

". . . and obviously, I can't just drop everything and head off to New York next week," Mrs Montez was saying into the phone. "We'll have to push back this move to next month at the earliest. Especially since I'll have to make arrangements with my daughter's school, and . . ."

Gabriella's eyes widened. Slapping one hand over her mouth to cover her gasp, she backed quickly out of the room before her mother could see her. Out in the hall, she leaned against the wall trying to make sense of what she'd just heard.

It sounded as if her mother was talking about moving again!

CHAPTER THREE

"Troy! Troy Bolton! Wait up!"

Troy had barely set foot inside East High on Monday morning when he saw Hannah, the cute, dark-haired girl from his algebra class, running towards him. Well, maybe not *running* exactly – more like half running and half hopping. The fuzzy pink bedroom slippers she was wearing kept slipping off as she rushed across the school lobby. Today was Pyjama Day, the first day of Spirit Week, and East High looked like a giant slumber party.

“What’s up, Hannah?” Troy said, tugging at the shirt hem of his own checked flannel PJs. It definitely felt weird to wear his pyjamas to school. But it was kind of fun, too. “Ready for that algebra quiz today?”

“Yeah,” Hannah said breathlessly. “I mean, no. I mean, who cares? I have something much more important to talk to you about. Will you go to the dance with me?”

Troy gulped. “Oh, wow,” he said, stalling for time. Hannah was the fourth girl to ask him so far. There was Ami yesterday, and then two more girls had called last night. Not Gabriella, though . . . and even after all that practice saying no, Troy still wasn’t sure what to say now that another girl was asking. “Um, I’m totally flattered. But I’m sort of planning to go with someone else.”

“So I’m too late?” Hannah cried. “You already said yes to someone?”

“Sort of. Well, not really. I mean, I’m waiting for that to happen.” Troy shrugged, feeling stupid. "That is, I'm expecting someone to ask me soon, but she hasn't quite yet. But I'm already sort of planning to, you know, say yes to her. So it's sort of like I already have, right?"

"Oh." Hannah looked crestfallen – and a little confused. "Okay."

"Excuse me!" They were both distracted by a loud voice coming from the direction of the front door. "Coming through."

Troy glanced over. His eyes widened as he saw Sharpay striding into the lobby. She was wearing a pair of bright red silk pyjamas with little Wildcats logos printed all over them. On her feet, she wore leather slippers shaped like a pair of snarling wildcats. Spotting Troy, Sharpay waved and then marched right up to him, pushing Hannah out of her way.

"Pardon me, Heidi," Sharpay said. "I have something *tres* important to discuss with Troy." She shot the other girl a quick smile. For all her acting skills, Troy thought, it didn't look terribly convincing. "I'm sure you understand."

"My name is Hannah," Hannah said.

Sharpay had already turned towards Troy. At Hannah's response, she turned back and blinked at her. "Um, are you still here?" Without waiting for an answer, she spun back to smile at Troy. "Good morning, Troy. I love your pyjamas."

Troy glanced at Hannah out of the corner of his eye as she rolled her eyes and stomped away, her fuzzy slippers slapping the tile floor.

"I like yours, too, Sharpay," he said. "Very spirited."

"Thank you." Sharpay smoothed down her pyjama top, looking pleased with herself. "I had them custom made. The slippers, too. Aren't they absolutely adorable?" She held up one foot so Troy could admire it.

Just then, Troy noticed a huge, fuzzy creature shuffling towards them. It was covered in beige fur and was wearing a Wildcats team tank top. Only a pair of greyish blue eyes showed that there was a human inside. And those eyes looked sort of familiar . . .

"Ryan?" Troy said, peering past a shiny black rubber nose and a set of pipe-cleaner whiskers. "Is that you, man?"

"It's me," a miserable-sounding voice emerged from the mound of fur.

"Um . . . so is that really what you wear to sleep in?" Troy asked. Ryan could be a little eccentric. But this . . . ?

"Of course not," Sharpay answered for her brother. "He's part of my outfit. He's a stuffed Wildcat. Kind of like my own giant stuffed animal. It's Pyjamas Day. Get it?"

Troy grinned. Leave it to Sharpay to go over the top, even on something as simple as Pyjamas Day.

"O-o-okay," he said. "Lookin' good, man." He clapped Ryan on the shoulder.

Guess Sharpay's already angling for that Spirit Queen title, he thought. And we all know that when Sharpay wants something, she really goes for it!

"So, Troy," Sharpay said. "Do you have a date for the Spirit Ball yet? Because it just so happens that I'm still–"

"Excuse me," Troy interrupted. He'd just spotted Gabriella walking in through the school doors. "I'll be right back, okay?"

"But I was just about to–"

Once again, he didn't let Sharpay finish her sentence. He took off towards Gabriella.

Gabriella was barely aware of the usual Monday-morning pre-tutor group commotion all around her as she moved across the crowded lobby. She was thinking about what she'd overheard in the kitchen the afternoon before. In fact, she hadn't thought about much else since it happened. She'd almost forgotten it was Pyjamas Day – luckily she'd remembered just in time, pulling on a pale blue nightgown and her favourite ballet-style slippers.

How could Mum even think about moving again? she asked herself for what had to be the 50th time. She promised she wouldn't do that to me. Not this time. This time, we were supposed to be here to stay.

"Gabriella!"

She snapped out of it when she realized that Troy was hurrying towards her, waving and calling her name. Forcing a smile, she returned his wave.

"Nice pyjamas," she said as he skidded to a stop in front of her.

"Thanks. Yours, too."

There was a moment of silence. Gabriella immediately drifted back to her earlier thoughts. Could it really be true? Could she be leaving East High so soon?

The trouble was, she still didn't know for sure. All she had to go on was that overheard phone call. Normally she had no trouble talking to her mother about anything. But this was different somehow. Maybe it was because she really didn't want to know the answer . . .

"Gabriella? Did you hear me?"

Once again, Gabriella snapped back to the

here and now. "Sorry, Troy," she said. "Um, I guess it's kind of loud in here. What did you say?"

"I said, I wonder if Sharpay is going to bring a live wildcat as her date to the Spirit Ball to make sure she wins that Spirit Queen title." Troy laughed. "I can't wait to go to the dance and see, can you?"

"Um, sure. I mean, I can't wait either." Gabriella really didn't care what Sharpay did at that weekend's dance. She was much more concerned about whether she, herself, would ever get to attend another dance at East High. For a second she was tempted to share her worries with Troy. "Um, listen, Troy . . ."

But she stopped herself just in time, biting her tongue. What was she thinking?

"What is it?" Troy took a step closer, staring at her intently.

Gabriella shook her head. "Nothing." She couldn't believe she'd almost blurted out what she was thinking. Why ruin Troy's Spirit Week with such depressing news? "I mean, ah,

I was just going to say I liked your slippers."

"Oh." Troy glanced down at his own feet before meeting her eyes again. "Because for a second there, I thought you were going to–"

"Troy!" Sharpay came barging over, cutting him off in mid-sentence. "So *here's* where you disappeared to – didn't you promise you'd be right back?" She arranged her face into a playful pout. "And I *really* need to talk to you about something – in *private*."

For once, Gabriella didn't mind when Sharpay dragged Troy away. She was too distracted to talk to anybody at the moment, anyway. Even Troy.

I need to get a handle on this somehow, she thought. Otherwise my Spirit Week will be ruined – and my friends' week, too. And we should probably enjoy it as much as possible, considering it may be the last one we all have together.

She hurried out of the lobby and down the hall. On the way to her tutor room, she passed the school hall. The doors were open, and she heard the sounds of thumping and banging.

Gabriella paused and glanced inside. She immediately recognized Kelsi Nielsen, the composer of the winter musical. Kelsi was struggling to lift a large piece of red-and-black–striped plywood. As Gabriella watched, Kelsi finally got the piece of wood off the ground – and almost fell off the edge of the stage. At the last second, she let go of the wood, which went crashing to the floor.

"Are you okay?" Gabriella cried, hurrying towards her.

Kelsi jumped at Gabriella's words, almost falling off the stage again. "Oh! Hi, Gabriella," she said in her soft, shy voice. She shoved her wire-rimmed glasses back up her nose. "I didn't see you come in."

"What are you doing?" Gabriella glanced around the hall. It looked like it always did when the drama club was in the midst of a scenery-painting frenzy – sheets of plywood, paint cans and other bits of equipment were littered everywhere. "Is there another musical coming up that I didn't hear about?"

Kelsi smiled and mopped a few beads of sweat from her forehead with the back of her hand. "Nothing like that," she said. "This is for the dance on Saturday. Ms Darbus is in charge of decorating and she wants the place to, um, glitter and pop like the set of the Oscars."

Gabriella laughed. "That sounds like Ms Darbus!" she said, thinking of the school's drama teacher. She also realized with a twinge of guilt that she hadn't asked Troy to the dance yet. "And it also sounds like too big a job for one person. Need some help?"

"Thanks," Kelsi said gratefully. "Now that you mention it . . ."

Gabriella dropped her bag on a chair and hurried forward to grab one end of the plywood sheet. Kelsi wasn't the type of person to ask for help unless she was really desperate. She just stepped up and did what needed to be done. Gabriella figured the least she could do was help her out this time. Besides, Kelsi was good at keeping secrets. If Gabriella confided in her about what she'd overheard, maybe she could get some advice about her problem . . .

CHAPTER FOUR

"Check it out!" somebody cried in the crowded school lobby the next morning. "Sharpay has a house on her head!"

Troy glanced up from talking with his buddies just in time to see Sharpay marching proudly through the front door. His jaw dropped in amazement. She had an enormous contraption balanced precariously on top of her head. It appeared to be some kind of mutant doll's house that she had attached to a large hat.

"What *is* that thing?" somebody asked Sharpay loudly.

She stopped in the middle of the room and struck a pose. "Isn't it obvious?" she asked, her stage-trained voice carrying to every corner of the lobby. "It's my hat for Hat Day, of course! It's a scale model of our own beloved East High. See?" She lifted one hand and pointed carefully at something at the top of the structure on her head. "That's me on the roof, waving the school flag."

Troy ducked behind Zeke as Sharpay turned on her heels, the edifice on top of her head wobbling as she glanced around. She seemed to be looking for someone, and he didn't want her to spot him. Sharpay had asked him to the dance twice the day before, including the time she'd dragged him away from Gabriella before tutor room. Troy definitely didn't want to have to find a new, even more creative way to turn her down yet again.

"Whoa," Chad said, still staring at Sharpay.

"Somebody should tell that girl today is *Hat* Day, not Pile-everything-but-the-kitchen-sink-on-your-head Day."

Jason was grinning. "Good thing her neck is already used to carrying her big, swelled head around," he joked. "Otherwise, it would snap in two under all that weight."

Troy chuckled, but he wasn't paying that much attention. He had been keeping an eye out for Gabriella since arriving at school and he'd just spotted her entering the lobby.

"Catch you later, guys," he told his teammates. Then he jogged over to Gabriella. "Hey!" he greeted her. "Nice hat."

Gabriella reached up and touched the brim of the plain blue baseball cap she was wearing. "Not really," she said with a laugh. "I almost forgot today was Hat Day. This was the best I could find at short notice."

"Really? In that case, here." Troy grabbed his own hat, a cool striped top hat. "We can swap."

"No, really. That's okay," Gabriella protested.

"I insist." Troy pushed his hat into her hands. "You don't want to look like a chump for the tutor room hat parade, do you?" He laughed. "Especially after the humiliation of watching Chad win that Best Pyjamas award yesterday."

Gabriella grinned. Somehow, even when she was feeling down, Troy could make her feel at least a little bit better.

"Thanks," she said, making the trade. She put on his striped hat. It was a tad big, but it still felt good. "And don't worry – if I win that Hat award, I won't forget to thank you in my acceptance speech."

"Deal." Troy smiled at her and didn't say anything else. He just stood there with her baseball cap in his hands, waiting for her to say something else.

Gabriella cleared her throat nervously. She wondered if he could tell there was something up with her lately. Sharing her secret with Kelsi yesterday had made her feel better for a little while, but today her worries were back at full strength. I really haven't been acting like myself, she thought. I'm sure he can tell there's something bugging me this week.

"So . . ." Troy said after a long moment of silence. "Is there anything you–"

Before he could finish, the bell rang to call everyone to their tutor rooms.

"Oops, we'd better get moving," Gabriella said, relieved to be saved by the bell. She reached up to pat the hat on her head. "I don't want to waste this baby by missing that parade."

By the time the final bell rang, Troy was starting to wonder if he was living in a parallel universe – one where Gabriella Montez didn't have any intention of asking him to the Spirit Ball. Because no matter how many times he managed to run into her between classes and how many hints he dropped, she still hadn't said a word about it.

"She ask you yet, bro?" Chad asked him as they met up at their lockers before basketball practice.

Troy shook his head and sighed. "Nope," he said. "But Susan Kane did. So did Ashley Ramirez."

"What about Sharpay?" Chad asked.

Troy rolled his eyes. "Yeah, her, too," he said. "Three times."

"That girl doesn't know how to take no for an answer!" Chad laughed. "You should've heard her arguing with Ms Darbus after she awarded Best Hat to Cyndra this morning. I'm telling you, Sharpay is wasted here in high school – she should be on the Supreme Court or something!"

Troy chuckled, but he wasn't all that amused. He was getting tired of saying no to other girls. What was Gabriella waiting for? When was she going to ask him? Or *was* she? He was really starting to wonder.

"Ready to hit the gym, bro?" Chad asked, slamming his locker shut. "Practice starts in 20."

"I'll meet you there," Troy said.

He lingered by his locker for a while after

Chad left, then wandered down the hall looking for Gabriella. Despite his doubts, he wasn't ready to give up yet. Maybe she was just too shy to ask him out in front of other people. If he could just get her alone for a few minutes, maybe drop a few more subtle hints . . .

By the time Troy gave up on finding Gabriella, the halls of East High were silent and empty. Everybody had already left school or disappeared into their meetings, practices and rehearsals. Troy put on a burst of speed as he neared the gym. He knew Principal Matsui would get on his case if he caught him running in the halls. But he was less worried about that than he was about what his father would say if he was late.

Luckily he made it into the gym just seconds before his dad blew the whistle to start practice. Chad nudged him.

"Where's Zeke?" he whispered. "Did you see him on your way in?"

Troy merely shook his head, shooting his dad a glance out of the corner of his eye. As he did, he saw Zeke come skidding into the gym, out of breath and covered with a white substance that looked suspiciously like flour.

Coach Bolton saw him, too. "Glad you could join us, Mr Baylor," he said sarcastically.

"Sorry, Coach." Zeke panted, doing his best to brush himself off. "Lost track of time. Won't happen again."

"See that it doesn't."

Zeke jogged over and joined the other guys. "What's with you, man?" Jason whispered.

"The clock in the home-ec lab is slow," Zeke whispered back.

"The home-ec lab?" Chad rolled his eyes. "Man, you are spending *way* too much time in that place!"

Troy was surprised, too. It wasn't long ago that they'd all learned Zeke's secret – he loved to bake. In his spare time, he made all sorts of cakes, cookies, pies and pastries – and his crème brûlée was already the stuff of legend. But being late for practice because he was baking after school? That wasn't like him.

"So what's the deal?" Jason asked. "You planning to quit the Wildcats and start the East High pastry team?"

"Nothing like that." Zeke shook his head. "It's because of Spirit Week. I've been helping out, making cookies and stuff for the ball on Saturday. I just took a whole batch of Wildcat cookies out of the oven."

Troy's stomach rumbled. He'd been so busy talking to Gabriella and dropping hints about the dance at lunchtime that he'd barely eaten anything. A few of Zeke's cookies sounded good just about now . . . "That's cool," he said, licking his lips. "Can't wait to taste one."

"Yeah, right. Won't be so cool if we lose the game 'cause Zeke's thinking harder about icing than free throws," Chad put in. "You gotta keep your head in the game, man!"

"You don't have to worry about me," Zeke said quickly. "I'll be there, 150 per cent. Oh! But wait until you guys see the special cookies I'm designing for the Spirit King and Queen. They're shaped like little crowns – get it? For king and queen?" He grinned proudly, absent-mindedly brushing flour off his arm. "It took me a while to figure out how to make them look like they were made out of gold, though." He elbowed Troy and winked. "I hope you like banana icing, Your Majesty."

A sharp whistle interrupted them. "Hey!" Coach Bolton barked. "Enough talking. Are you boys on the Wildcats or the gossip squad?"

"Wildcats!" Jason, Chad and Zeke yelled.

Troy pumped his fist. "Go, Wildcats!" he added.

"Good." His father looked satisfied. "Then let's start that new layup drill we did last time. Let me see you hustle!"

CHAPTER FIVE

"Hey, Gabriella! Where's your twin?" someone yelled as Gabriella stepped off the school bus on Wednesday morning.

Gabriella smiled weakly at the girl who'd asked. "Only child here," she quipped. "No twin for me."

She hurried on towards the door before the girl could ask any more questions. The girl shrugged, turning to whisper something to the 'twin' standing next to her. Both of them were dressed in jeans and pink sweaters, and they had matching scarves tied around their necks.

I'm *so* not in the mood for this, Gabriella thought, glancing around. Everywhere she looked, she saw double. It was Twin Day, and people were going all out, just as they had for Pyjamas Day and Hat Day.

Gabriella knew it was her own fault that she looked out of place. Both Troy and Taylor had asked her to be their twin. But Gabriella had turned down both of them. She was too worried about the whole moving thing to think about something as silly as matching clothes.

Instead, she'd been spending every spare moment wondering how she could have been stupid enough to believe she was really at East High to stay. How many times had she been through this? True, those other times her mother hadn't made any promises. But still, hadn't she just been thinking about how hard her mother was working lately? Sort of the way she always did when she was preparing for another big promotion . . . ?

Anyway, Gabriella thought as she dodged several more sets of twins, if I'm going to be starting at another new school soon, I might as well get used to feeling like the odd one out. Because there's no way I'll ever feel as at home at another school as I do at this one . . .

At that same moment, Troy was wandering down the hall towards the tutor room, feeling a little out of place in a school full of matching outfits. He broke into a smile when he spotted Chad loping towards him. He looked just like he did every day – dressed in jeans and a T-shirt, with a basketball tucked under one arm.

"Yo, there you are!" Troy exclaimed, hurrying over to trade high fives with his friend. "I was starting to think I was the only one in the entire school without a twin. Looks like you're on your own, too, huh? Want to change into our team shirts or something so we'll match up?"

"Sorry, bro." Chad shook his head. "I've already got a twin."

"You do? Who?" Troy asked in surprise. He knew Zeke and Jason had decided to pair up and the rest of the team was spoken for, too.

"Taylor. I'm supposed to be meeting her by her locker right now – she brought a hat for me to wear or something."

Troy felt his heart sink. He'd tried to call Chad last night after Gabriella had said no to being his twin. But the line had been busy for over an hour and finally he'd given up. Now he realized his friend must have been talking to Taylor.

"So does this mean you guys are cool again?" he asked. "Last I heard, she was still mad at you for acting like such a dork the other day at the mall."

Chad shrugged sheepishly. "She's still kind of mad," he said. "But since Gabriella didn't want to be her twin, she decided I would have to do." He spun his basketball on the tip of one finger. "I figure it'll give me the perfect chance to win her over again with my charm and wit."

Troy was glad to hear that the two of them

were on their way to making up after their fight. But this meant he really was on his own today.

"Oh, well," he said, trying not to sound too disappointed. "Looks like I'm just going to have to be the guy without a twin all day." He held up his hands as if framing a picture. "Sounds like a made-for-TV movie, doesn't it? *The Guy Without a Twin.*"

"Yoo-hoo, Troy!" Sharpay rushed up to them. "Did I just hear you say you don't have a twin?"

Troy winced, wishing he'd kept his voice down. Chad grinned and faded away into the crowd. "That's right, Sharpay," Troy said. "I'm afraid I'm twinless. Looks like you and Ryan have your act together as usual, though."

Sharpay shot a glance at her brother, who was right behind her. Both of them were wearing black trousers with rhinestones down the sides, silky white shirts, red bolero jackets and jaunty red hats with black feathers. When Ryan turned for a second to brush a speck of lint off his trousers, Troy saw that there was a Wildcats logo on the back of his jacket, outlined in black and silver glitter.

"Oh. Right." Sharpay shrugged, then turned to smile at Troy. "But I'm sure Ryan wouldn't mind if you took his place. After all, we can't have the Captain of the basketball team and the future Spirit King of East High . . ." She paused just long enough to give an obvious wink and smirk. ". . . without a twin for Twin Day! That just wouldn't look right."

"Oh, I don't know . . ." Troy began.

Sharpay rested one hand on his arm, smiling up at him. "You don't have to thank me," she said. "It would be an honour to be your twin. In fact, it gives us a chance to practise looking good together – you know, for when we're crowned on Saturday night." She tapped her chin with one finger, which Troy noticed was manicured in matching red with black glitter. "Come to think of it, the whole spirit-royalty thing gives us all the more reason to go to the ball together. Want to reconsider?"

Troy opened his mouth to say no again, then hesitated. Was he making a fool of himself by waiting around for Gabriella to ask him to the dance? Maybe she wasn't planning to ask him at all. What would he do then? Aside from Sharpay, all the other girls who'd asked him had gone ahead and asked other guys. And he was going to look like the world's biggest loser if he was the only one on the team without a date.

But as far as he knew, Gabriella hadn't asked anyone else. That meant there was still hope. Didn't it?

He shook his head firmly, trying to ignore his doubts. "I already told you, Sharpay. I don't think that's a good idea."

"Really? Because a little birdie told me you still don't have a date. And if there's one thing worse than a Spirit King without a twin . . . well, whatever." Sharpay flicked her fingers, as if shooing away a pesky fly. "Now, why don't you and Ryan go into the little boys' room and trade outfits?"

Ryan cleared his throat, looking anxious. "Wait – maybe we could all be triplets instead," he suggested. "I'm sure we could find Troy a matching outfit in the Drama Club costume cupboard."

"Triplets?" Sharpay rolled her eyes. "I think not. Didn't you ever hear the saying 'three's a crowd'?" She turned back towards Troy. "Now, Troy, about the dance . . ."

"Come on, Ryan," Troy said quickly. "Let's go switch outfits."

He wasn't exactly thrilled about walking around school looking like a matador who had fallen into a vat of glitter. But he decided it was a small price to pay to get Sharpay to shut up about the dance for a while. He needed to figure out what to do about Gabriella.

By the time Troy emerged from the men's room, he had come up with a plan.

It's like when we're two points behind with a minute to go, he thought, adjusting his hat so he *could see past its droopy black feather. There's no more time to mess around. I need to grab the ball and make a drive for the basket – er, I mean, find Gabriella and just come out and ask her if she's ever planning to ask me to that dance.*

Having reached that decision, he already felt a little bit better. He was used to being a play-maker on the basketball team. Was this sort of situation really that different?

"See you later, dude," Troy told Ryan, who seemed a bit disgruntled as he stared down at the faded blue jeans and grey hoodie he was now wearing. "I need to, um, run an errand."

He took off without waiting for an answer, heading straight to Ms Darbus's tutor room to see if Gabriella was there yet. She wasn't, though Taylor was, tapping her foot and staring at her watch.

"Troy!" she exclaimed when she spotted him. "Have you seen Chad?"

"Yeah, a few minutes ago," Troy said distractedly as he glanced around the room. Only a few students were there this early. "He was going to meet you at your locker. Have you seen Gabriella?"

"At my locker?" Taylor cried, throwing both hands in the air. "What's wrong with that boy? I *told* him to meet me *here*!"

She stomped towards the door, brushing past Troy on her way. "Taylor!" he called urgently. "Gabriella – do you know where she is?"

"Oh!" Taylor paused, shooting him an apologetic smile. "Nope, sorry. Haven't seen her."

Troy sighed as Taylor disappeared through the classroom door. He turned and followed her out, rushing through the halls in search of Gabriella. She wasn't at her locker. There was no sign of her in the chemistry lab. And when he stuck his head into the school hall, the only people in sight were Kelsi and Zeke.

"Hi, Troy!" Zeke waved a paintbrush at him. "Did you come to help us work on decorations for the dance? I told Kelsi I'd help her while my latest batch of cookies is cooling."

"Maybe later, okay?" Troy was so distracted that he barely took in what his team-mate was saying. "Uh, Gabriella hasn't been here, has she?"

"Nope, not today," Kelsi replied, dipping her paintbrush into a bucket of red paint.

"Okay, thanks anyway. See you."

It was only when Troy found himself back in the lobby that he finally spotted Gabriella. She was standing with Ryan, laughing as he fiddled with something in her hair.

"Gabriella!" Troy cried.

Gabriella looked up when she heard Troy calling her name. Her laugh froze on her lips. He was dressed in some kind of ridiculous outfit that looked a couple of sizes too small for him. But even so, he still looked cute.

For a few minutes, Ryan had actually helped her forget about her problems. Upon discovering that she, like he, was twinless for the day, he'd insisted they pair up for the twin parade, even though the only thing their outfits had in common was that they were both wearing jeans. They'd had a great time putting together a silly costume consisting mostly of gym-towel capes and folded-newspaper hats.

But seeing Troy suddenly brought all her worries flooding back. How was she ever going to say goodbye to him?

He skidded to a stop in front of her. "Nice outfit," she told him, forcing a smile. "Very, um, dashing."

"Yeah, thanks." He grimaced and glanced down at himself, tugging at the hem of his glittery red jacket. "But never mind that – I really need to talk to you about something."

The expression on his face was so earnest and open that Gabriella felt like crying. This was ridiculous – she needed to tell him the truth about why she was acting so weird this week.

No, she thought firmly. It's bad enough that my Spirit Week is practically ruined. I can't ruin his, too. Or anybody else's, for that matter. I probably shouldn't even have told Kelsi; it was totally selfish of me to lay my bad news on her. But at least I swore her to secrecy so she won't tell anyone else and get them down, too. I can tell them all the truth next week – that's soon enough.

"Gabriella?" Troy said. "Are you okay?"

Just then the PA system crackled to life. Principal Matsui came on, announcing that the twin parade was about to start.

"Come on!" Ryan exclaimed, adjusting his cape. "We need to get a spot near the front if we want to have any chance of winning this thing."

Gabriella shot Troy an apologetic glance. "Sorry, I have to go," she said.

Grabbing Ryan by the hand, she took off with him towards the front of the parade.

CHAPTER SIX

"Hold still, Gabriella. I need to pin this and I don't want to poke you in the side."

Gabriella held her breath and stood as still as she could while her mother fiddled with the old-fashioned dress she was wearing. *I think Mum is more enthusiastic about this Historical Character Day costume than I am,* she thought, biting back a sigh.

"You didn't have to go to all this trouble," Gabriella said. "I'll just have a lab coat on over the dress, anyway."

"It's no problem." Her mother grabbed one of the pins she was holding in her mouth. "I want you to be the most accurate little Marie Curie you can be! Now keep still."

Gabriella smiled weakly and went back to holding her breath. She stared at the top of her mother's head, wishing she knew what thoughts were going on inside her brain. Was she thinking about the next big move? Trying to figure out how long it would take to find a new house in New York? Deciding when and how to break the news? *Maybe she's doing the same thing I'm doing with my friends,* Gabriella thought, *waiting until after Spirit Week to deliver the blow.*

Chewing her lower lip, Gabriella allowed her eyes to wander up and around her room, taking in the photos of her friends tucked into the mirror frame and the East High banner pinned to her bulletin board. This was the perfect time to ask her mother about that overheard phone conversation. But she just couldn't bear to do it right now. It was just too hard to think about leaving, especially this week, when everyone was so pumped up with school spirit. Knowing for sure that it was really happening would just be too much. If her mother confirmed that they were moving, Gabriella knew she would never be able to hide her feelings from her friends. And she was still determined not to ruin their Spirit Week with her bad news.

"There," her mother said, stepping back and brushing off her hands as she surveyed Gabriella's costume. "Now you look exactly like a turn-of-the-century Nobel-prize-winning physicist." She laughed. "Maybe I need to start looking for a side job designing Broadway costumes or something!"

Gabriella gasped, feeling as if she'd just been punched in the stomach. Broadway costumes? Broadway was in New York City. Why would her mother mention Broadway right now? It seemed her earlier speculation might be true after all; her mother *did* have New York on her mind . . .

"What's wrong?" Her mother immediately looked concerned.

"N-nothing," Gabriella stammered, doing her best to regain her composure. "I – uh – I just remembered I told Taylor I'd meet her before tutor group to help her with her outfit. I'm going to be late."

She yanked on her lab coat and rushed out of her room. She might as well accept the truth: she would be leaving again soon. All she could do was just try to enjoy whatever time she had left at East High.

Gabriella suddenly realized that the dance was only two days away. *I'm going to ask Troy to the Spirit Ball today,* she thought. *No more distractions.*

When she entered the school lobby a short while later, she looked around for Troy. Instead she spotted Sharpay and Ryan, who were dressed in what appeared to be authentic formal attire from the early 20th century.

Sharpay spotted Gabriella, too. She hurried towards her, her long skirt rustling.

"Let me guess – Madam Curie, right?" Sharpay said. "Cute. I played her in a musical once."

Ryan nodded. "Sharpay gave a fabulous performance. Very convincing."

"So who are you two supposed to be?" Gabriella asked, hoping it wasn't a rude question.

"I'm glad you asked." Sharpay raised her voice, glancing over at Principal Matsui, who happened to be passing by, as if hoping he would overhear. "We're dressed as Susannah and Jonathan Smith, the founders of East High."

"It wasn't my idea," Ryan put in with a shrug. "I was planning to come as Charlie Chaplin."

Sharpay shot him a slightly irritated glance. "That's right, it was *my* idea," she said, even more loudly. "Since this is supposed to be *Spirit* Week, I thought it would be nice to celebrate our school *spirit* by – hey!" she interrupted herself, jumping back as Chad and Jason almost crashed into her. They were racing through the school lobby, clowning around and tossing punches at each other. Both of them were dressed as Abraham Lincoln. "Watch it, you maniacs!" Sharpay cried. "This dress happens to be a very delicate historical artefact."

"Sorr-ry!" Chad said, giving Jason one last shove and then turning to stare at Sharpay and Ryan. He wrinkled his nose and sniffed. "It sure *smells* like a historical artefact."

Jason laughed. "Yeah – and all that historical dust is making me want to sneeze!"

"Hmmph!" Sharpay spun on her heels and turned up her nose.

Gabriella wasn't sure whether to laugh or roll her eyes. Before she could do either, she noticed Kelsi coming down the hall, struggling beneath the weight of a huge roll of red-and-black fabric.

"Hey! Careful with that." Gabriella rushed over and grabbed one end of the fabric roll.

"Thanks," Kelsi panted. "It *is* kind of heavy.

But I really need to start taking stuff over to the gym. There's still a ton to do to get ready for tomorrow's pep rally. Zeke is supposed to be helping, but there was some kind of oven emergency, so . . ."

"Say no more," Gabriella said. "We'll all help you. Right, guys?" She glanced at Sharpay and Ryan.

"Are you kidding?" Sharpay cried. "Didn't you just hear me say that our costumes are historical artefacts? They're very fragile. We had to, like, sign papers before they'd let us rent them from the history museum."

"Hey, guys. What's going on?"

Gabriella turned to see Troy, dressed as Mark Twain, walking up to them. "Hi!" she said, blushing a little as she remembered why she'd been looking for him.

He smiled at her, then glanced at Kelsi. "Looks like you could use some help," he said, grabbing Gabriella's end of the fabric roll. "Where are we taking this?"

"Thanks, Troy," Kelsi said. "This way . . ."

Gabriella started to go along with them. This could be the perfect opportunity to ask Troy to the dance – as soon as they were out of the lobby, that is. She didn't mind asking him in front of Kelsi, but she wasn't crazy about doing it in front of Sharpay and Ryan, too.

But before she'd taken more than three steps, she felt someone grab her arm and yank her back. It was Sharpay.

"It's totally working!" Sharpay whispered, widening her eyes dramatically.

"What's working?" Gabriella asked. She glanced over her shoulder. Troy and Kelsi were already halfway down the hall.

Sharpay dropped her grip on Gabriella's arm and clasped her hands together. "Didn't you see the way Troy just smiled at you?" she exclaimed. "I can tell you've been playing it cool like I advised. He's definitely appreciating you more – it totally shows!"

"Huh?" Gabriella blinked, suddenly remembering their conversation the previous Friday afternoon. "Oh – really?"

"Uh-huh." Sharpay smiled and winked broadly. "Keep up the good work and you'll have him eating out of your hand. Toodles!" She waved and hurried off.

Gabriella turned to look for Troy and Kelsi, but they had already disappeared from sight around the corner of the hall. Gabriella was about to follow, but just then Principal Matsui came on the PA system, calling everyone to the lobby for the historical-costume parade.

"Rats," Gabriella muttered as kids started pouring into the lobby from all directions. She spotted Taylor coming in, dressed as Cleopatra. "I need to talk to you about something," Gabriella said, pulling her aside. She glanced around to make sure nobody else was listening. "It's about Troy."

"What about him?"

Gabriella noticed that Taylor didn't sound very interested. In fact, she was sort of scowling. But there were only a few moments before the parade started, so she continued.

"You know I've been planning all week to ask him to the dance, right?" Gabriella said. "Well, remember how Sharpay told me I should play it cool, not seem too eager? I just saw her and she thinks that's what I've been doing – and she thinks it's working! She says it's making Troy appreciate me more, or something . . ." She took a deep breath. "So I guess what I'm asking is, do you think she could possibly be right?"

Taylor shrugged, her scowl deepening. "How should I know?" she snapped. "I'm the last person you should ask about guys. As far as I'm concerned, they all stink!"

"What?" Gabriella blinked in surprise. "Wait, I thought you and Chad made up on Twin Day."

"I thought so, too." Taylor tossed her head. "So then why did he still refuse to give me a straight answer about the dance when I asked him just now?"

She spun on her heels and marched into the

classroom. Gabriella watched her go, feeling helpless. Why was it that the most complex chemistry equation was a piece of cake for her, yet she couldn't seem to figure out why anybody did anything?

CHAPTER SEVEN

"Go Wildcats!" Troy whooped as he bounded into the gym with his team-mates the next day. It was time for the lunchtime pep rally and he couldn't wait! It was the perfect way to get the whole team psyched up for Saturday's game.

At least half the student body was already seated in the bleachers. They let out a cheer at Troy's entrance. Troy grinned and gave the entire gym a thumbs-up.

"This is going to be fun," Jason commented.

"Yeah," Chad agreed. "But why couldn't we have the pep rally during fourth period instead of lunch hour? I think I just failed that chemistry test."

"Don't think about that, man," another teammate advised. "Think about winning tomorrow!"

"Where's Zeke?" Jason asked as the guys made their way towards the section of bleachers reserved for them.

Chad shrugged, glancing around the gym. "Probably up to his elbows in cookie dough, the way he's been all week," he said. "I swear, the dude is making sure there will be at least a dozen cookies for every person at that dance."

Troy was still looking around, too, but not for Zeke. He was searching for Gabriella. But she was nowhere to be seen.

When they reached their seats, Sharpay was already sitting in the row of bleachers directly behind them. Sharpay waved at the team members.

"Here come our little school heroes now," she

cooed. "Ready for the game tomorrow, boys?"

Troy grinned as he took in her outfit. It was School Colours Day and Sharpay was decked out in Wildcats red and black from head to toe – literally. She'd dyed her blonde hair bright red. Her lips were a matching scarlet and thick smudges of black eyeliner ringed her eyes. Her shirt was red, her trousers glossy black and her high-heeled black shoes had little red bows on them. At first Troy thought her bright-red fingernails were smudged, but when he took a closer look, he saw that she'd painted tiny Wildcat logos on each nail.

"You're certainly showing your Wildcat spirit today, Sharpay," Troy commented, trying not to laugh.

"Is that what you call it?" Chad put in. "I would've guessed my dog just ate a box full of red and black crayons and then threw up on her." He grinned and traded high fives with Jason.

Sharpay smirked. "Very amusing – for a basketball Neanderthal, at least."

"So Sharpay, where's your brother?" Jason asked. "I can't wait to see what *he's* wearing."

Sharpay shrugged. "He'll be here soon," she said. "Gabriella stopped him on the way in. Said she had something very important to ask him."

"Oh." Something about the way Sharpay turned to stare at him suddenly made Troy feel a little queasy. What was that all about?

Before he could think about it too much, Ryan appeared in the doorway. He strode towards them, ignoring the commotion going on around him. Like his sister, he was dressed all in red and black, though he'd left his hair colour alone, settling for a jaunty red hat with a black feather. Troy was pretty sure it was the same one he'd borrowed on Twin Day.

"Hey Ryan, is Gabriella with you?" Troy asked when Ryan reached them. He craned his neck for a better look at the gym entrance, hoping to see her enter.

Ryan took a seat beside his sister and smoothed out the creases in his black trousers.

"She's on her way," he said. "I was just talking with her outside. Oh!" He turned to Sharpay, looking excited. "I also just saw Ms Falstaff. She mentioned how much she's enjoyed our outfits all week."

Sharpay clapped her hands. "Excellent!" she said. "That's one more vote for me." She patted her bright-red hair. "Not that I need it."

Chad rolled his eyes. "Be sure to let us know when you decide to run for national office, Sharpay."

"No thanks," Sharpay said. "I'll settle for East High Spirit Queen. At least for now." She leaned forward and touched Troy on the shoulder. "I'm really looking forward to it – especially to dancing with my king once we're crowned."

Troy grinned sheepishly as his team-mates whooped and whistled. "Yeah, okay," he said. "Um, me, too, I guess. But I'm looking forward to dancing with my *own* date, too."

"Dude!" Jason clapped him on the back. "Does that mean Gabriella finally asked you?"

Troy felt more sheepish than ever. In fact, he was pretty sure his cheeks were going as red as his Wildcats uniform. "Um, not exactly," he said. "Not yet, I mean. But I'm sure she will. Soon."

"Oh, really?" Sharpay stuck one hand out in front of herself, carefully studying her Wildcat fingernails. "I'm sure you're right, Troy. After all, there are still nearly 30 hours before the dance. And she *does* seem to be in an asking mood today – just ask my brother." She turned and winked at Ryan.

Ryan looked confused. "What do you mean, Sharpay?" he said. "Gabriella and I–"

"Don't need to tell everyone your business," Sharpay finished for him, hushing him with a finger to his lips.

Troy felt his heart stop. Was he going crazy, or was Sharpay implying that Gabriella had invited Ryan to be her date for the ball? Could that really be what she had wanted to ask him?

No way, he thought. Why would she ask *him*?

Then an image flashed into his mind, as vivid as if he'd seen it yesterday – because he had. It was the image of Gabriella standing with Ryan in the lobby before tutor group. Oh, sure, Sharpay and Kelsi had been there, too. But that wasn't all . . . there was the day before that, too, when he'd watched them run off together, hand in hand and laughing, dressed as twins. They certainly had seemed awfully chummy then . . .

Before he could come out and ask Ryan what was going on, Principal Matsui and Coach Bolton walked into the gym and the crowd let out a cheer. Troy turned around, staring out at the hectic pep-rally scene without really seeing any of it. This whole time, he'd thought about how humiliating it would be if Gabriella never asked him and he ended up without a date for the ball. But all along, he realized, he hadn't really believed it could happen. Not to him – not like this . . .

"Listen, Troy." Sharpay leaned forward, speaking directly into his ear. "I just want you to know, if you get tired of waiting around for a certain someone, my invitation still stands."

Troy gulped, glancing at her over his shoulder . . .

". . . so I guess we should meet tomorrow afternoon to do all the last-minute decorating," Gabriella said, feeling distracted. She was standing in the hallway outside the gym with Zeke and Kelsi. A muffled cheer burst out from inside – it sounded as if the pep rally was starting. "Ryan just promised he'd come and help out and ask Sharpay to come, too, so if we can get a few more people . . ."

"Cool," Zeke said, looking equally distracted. "Thanks for helping out. Come on, we'd better get in there."

The three of them raced down the hall towards the gym. Gabriella couldn't believe the day was already half over and she still hadn't asked Troy to the dance. Despite her determination, she'd never found another chance alone with him the day before. And he'd had to run off right after classes ended for an extra basketball practice.

I really should have called him last night after dinner, she thought.

But that hadn't quite happened, either. First she'd spent half an hour on the phone with Taylor, trying to convince her that she should give Chad another chance instead of staying home to do her chemistry homework on Saturday night. Then Kelsi called to see how she was holding up and the two of them had spent another half an hour on the phone.

Once Gabriella had hung up, her mother finally arrived home from work, looking ragged and exhausted. That had made Gabriella feel even more distracted by the whole moving situation, and by the time she remembered the dance it was too late to call Troy.

Oh, well, she thought, biting her lip. Troy's got to assume we're going together, right? Asking him is just a formality – even though it *feels* way scarier than that!

The gym was a madhouse when they entered. Principal Matsui was standing on the centre line with Coach Bolton, trying to adjust the microphone in front of them. The cheerleaders were nearby, bouncing around, doing one of their routines, and most of the students were clapping and cheering along.

Gabriella followed Zeke as he loped over towards the team bench. She smiled when she spotted Troy among the others. Most of his team-mates were jumping around or watching the cheerleaders, but he was still seated, twisting around to talk to someone behind him. When she got a little closer, Gabriella saw that he was talking to Sharpay.

Pushing her way past the excited cheerleaders, Gabriella finally reached the team bench. She took a deep breath, not wanting to miss yet another opportunity. Her heart was pounding, but she did her best to ignore that.

This only *seems* scary, she reminded herself.

It'll probably be sort of like that first duet Troy and I ever sang together – at first I thought I was going to throw up or at least faint. But once I got started, it was actually fun.

"Troy!" she blurted out, clambering over the bleacher seat. "I need to ask you something. Actually, it's something I've been meaning to ask you all week . . ."

"Huh?" he shouted over the noise of the crowd. Principal Matsui's microphone had just let out a loud whine of feedback, and most of the students were howling and stomping their feet on the bleachers in response. "I can't hear you!"

Gabriella cleared her throat and leaned closer. "I want to ask you something!" she cried. "Will you go to the Spirit Ball with me?"

She smiled, letting out a huge sigh of relief. Her guess had been right – once the words were out, it suddenly didn't seem so scary after all.

Then she noticed Troy's face. He was wearing

an expression of shock and confusion. Her smile faded. "What's wrong?" she asked.

Sharpay leaned forward.

"Sorry, Gabriella," she said with a smirk. "You're a little late to the party. See, Troy just agreed to go to the dance with me."

CHAPTER EIGHT

"All right, people, settle down." Ms Darbus clapped her hands for attention. "In case you've forgotten, this is still an institution of learning. And this is drama class, *not* how-to-behave-like-jungle-creatures class."

"Yo, how can we think about boring old drama stuff when we have a game to win tomorrow?" Chad cried, pumping his fist in the air. Several of the other students laughed and cheered.

Gabriella smiled along weakly. But she wasn't

in the mood for cheering. She was still stunned about Troy and Sharpay. Unfortunately, the pep rally had started right after Sharpay's announcement, so Gabriella hadn't been able to talk to Troy about it.

How could he do this? she wondered, glancing over her shoulder at him. To her surprise, he was staring back at her sombrely. Feeling her cheeks go pink, she quickly ducked her head and pretended to be very busy pulling her drama class notebook out of her bag.

When she looked up again, Ms Darbus was glaring at Chad. "All right, Mr Danforth," she said icily. "If you find my class so dull, perhaps a test on *The Taming of the Shrew* will get your attention, hmm?" She rolled the *r* in 'shrew' dramatically.

The entire class groaned. "No way, Ms D!" Zeke exclaimed. "We can't have a test during Spirit Week. It's just not – well – *spirited*!"

The drama teacher crossed her arms over the front of her flowing purple tunic. "That's *exactly* why we're having one," she said. "This whole school has become entirely too focused on tomorrow's silly sports contest. Pencils out, please and eyes on your own paper . . ."

Soon the classroom was silent as the students pored over their tests. Gabriella was usually one of the first ones to finish any test, but today she was having trouble focusing on the paper in front of her.

Like it's not bad enough that I'll be moving away soon, she thought, staring at a question on the test without really seeing it. Now I won't even get to enjoy my one and only Spirit Ball at East High.

She sighed, doodling a little Wildcat *W* in the margin of her paper. So much for the dance being her last big hurrah. If she wasn't going with Troy, she wasn't sure there was any point in going at all . . .

"*Wildcats, in the house!*"

Gabriella jumped, along with the rest of the class, as Sharpay suddenly leaped out of her seat and burst into a full-throated rendition of the school fight song. Ms Darbus was so startled that she nearly fell off her throne-like chair at the front of the room.

"Ms Evans!" she snapped, grasping the arms of her chair. "What is the meaning of this outburst?"

"Sorry, Ms Darbus," Sharpay said, not sounding sorry at all. "I guess I just got overwhelmed with school spirit for a minute there. You know – *Wildcats, in the house! Everybody say it now . . .*" Soon she was singing again.

Ms Darbus waved her hands in the air helplessly for several seconds before finally sputtering out, "Silence!"

Sharpay paused in her song. "Oh, was I doing it again?" she said sweetly. "I really just can't seem to control myself."

By now most of the class was sniggering. Gabriella rolled her eyes. Even in the distracted mood she'd been in all week, it had been impossible not to notice that Sharpay was campaigning hard for that Spirit Queen title.

That's probably why she wanted to go to the dance with Troy, she thought. He's sure to be named Spirit King and if there's one thing Sharpay adores it's a nice, neat, happy Broadway ending.

"I suggest you figure out how to control yourself, Ms Evans – immediately," Ms Darbus said, glaring at Sharpay. "Otherwise, you'll be able to sing to your heart's content in a special Saturday-night detention session tomorrow."

Sharpay immediately snapped her mouth shut and sat down. "Sorry," she said. "Won't happen again."

The rest of the class seemed to inch by at glacial speed. But finally the bell rang, releasing them. Gabriella gathered up her things quickly. She was pretty sure she'd failed that test, but she had bigger things on her mind. She needed to talk to Troy and find out why he'd agreed to go to the ball with Sharpay.

But she'd barely taken three steps out of

the room when Zeke caught up with her.

"Gabriella!" he panted, looking slightly panicky. "Can you help me? I need to carry a whole bunch of cookies down to the storage room before basketball practice starts."

Gabriella hesitated for only a split second. Then she nodded.

"Okay," she said, "lead the way."

Moments later they were tucking the cookies safely into big coolers in the storage room off the gym. Halfway back to the kitchen, Kelsi appeared in the doorway of the school hall, looking panicked.

"Do either of you have a spare second?" she asked. "We're trying to get the last few garlands woven so we can hang them up tomorrow, and we still need to paint that Wildcat cutout, but there are only four of us today, and . . ."

Gabriella glanced at Zeke, hoping he'd volunteer. Then she remembered that he had to rush off for basketball practice.

"I'll help," she said. "Just show me what to

do."

For the next hour or two, Kelsi and the rest of the decorations committee kept Gabriella busy weaving, painting and just generally helping out. When Zeke finally dashed back in, still dressed in his uniform, he looked delighted at their progress. "Gabriella, you're an angel for helping," Zeke told her. "I'll make sure you get all the cookies you can eat at the ball tomorrow night. Maybe I'll even make you a crème brûlée!"

"Thanks," Gabriella said with a smile. "But it's no problem, really. Besides, I'm not sure I'm even going to the ball."

"What?" Kelsi squeaked, looking shocked. "But you have to go! This isn't because of – um, *you* know – is it?" She bit her lip and shot a glance at Zeke.

Realizing she was referring to the moving secret, Gabriella quickly shook her head, not wanting Zeke to catch on. "I was planning to go," she said, "but since I don't have a date . . ."

"That's okay," Zeke said quickly. "I don't have

a date, either. I've been too busy baking and helping with the decorating stuff to even think about that sort of thing." He shrugged. "No big deal. Lots of people go stag."

"Yeah," Kelsi added. "I don't have a date, either. Maybe the three of us can go and hang out together?"

Gabriella hesitated. Both of them were staring at her with beseeching looks on their faces.

How can I say no? she thought. Especially after all the hard work they've put into this dance . . .

"Well . . . okay," she said at last. "That sounds like fun. It's a date." She laughed and rolled her eyes. "Or a non-date. Or whatever."

"Cool." Zeke smiled. "Now if you'll excuse me, my macaroons should be ready by now . . ."

By the time Gabriella made her escape, the school hallways were almost deserted. As she hurried towards the gym, she spotted a pair of guys from the team wandering along with towels slung over their shoulders.

"Hey!" she called to them. "Did everybody

leave practice already?"

"Uh-huh," one of the guys replied. "Like half an hour ago."

The other player nodded. "Coach wants us to go home and rest up for the big game."

"Oh." Gabriella slumped against the nearest row of lockers. "Um, good luck tomorrow."

So she was too late. No, she reminded herself, I was too late a couple of hours ago at that pep rally. Why make a big deal over it now? Troy and I can talk things out next week – *if* it still matters after everyone hears my other news.

"Yo, what's wrong with you, Troy?" Chad exclaimed. "That's the sixth free throw you've missed in a row!"

"Yeah," Jason added. He was sitting on the gym floor nearby watching Troy and Chad goof around after practice. The coach and the rest of the team had left a while ago, but the three of them were hanging out, waiting for Zeke to return from the kitchen. "You'd better play better than that tomorrow, or we're going to get slaughtered out there."

Troy sighed and jogged in to grab the rebound. "I know," he said. "I guess I just have a lot on my mind."

That was an understatement. He couldn't seem to stop thinking about the expression on Gabriella's face when she'd heard that he and Sharpay were going to the dance together. How could he have been so stupid? This whole time he'd been afraid that she didn't want to go with him. And now she thought *he* didn't want to go with *her*, when nothing could be further from the truth!

"Well, pull it together, man," Jason said. "The Spirit Ball isn't going to be much fun if we blow the big game tomorrow."

"I guess." Troy shrugged. "Actually, I was sort of thinking I might not go to the ball."

"What?" Chad's eyes widened. "What are you talking about? You have to go – you're going to be the Spirit King!"

Jason nodded, jumping to his feet and hurrying over to grab the ball out of Troy's hands. "Yeah, don't talk crazy, Troy!" he exclaimed. "You have to be there to witness my hot date with Ami the cheerleader."

Chad gave Jason a shove. "Give it up, man. You know you were her second choice." But his heart didn't seem to be in the teasing. He shot Troy a worried glance. "You're just kidding around about this, right? You wouldn't really skip the dance?"

Troy hesitated. His friends looked so worried and disappointed that he couldn't stand it. The last thing he wanted to do was mess things up further by upsetting his team-mates so they wouldn't play their best tomorrow.

"Sure, I was just joking around," he said. "Of course I'll go."

They laughed, looking relieved, and Troy forced a smile. I'll go, he thought. I just won't expect to have a good time.

CHAPTER NINE

BZZZZZT!

The final buzzer went off, ending the big game. The East High gymnasium erupted into wild cheers.

"We did it!" the cheerleaders howled, pompoms flashing as they leaped onto the court. "Wildcats, in the house!"

Troy grinned, glancing up at the scoreboard. HOME: 62, VISITORS: 54.

"Way to go, Captain!" Chad shouted, hurling himself at Troy and pounding him on the back. "Glad you got your groove back."

"Yeah, man. After yesterday, I was worried!" Jason joined them, jumping up and down and pumping his fist.

Troy spotted Zeke jogging towards them and raised both hands for a double high five. "Check it out, guys – here's our Man of the Match," he said. The score had been tied for most of the game until Zeke had made a big play, sinking two three-pointers in a row. After that the momentum had changed and it was all Wildcats.

Zeke grinned. "Thanks. But this win was a team effort – like always!"

Troy glanced at the stands, which were overflowing with excited Wildcats fans. Even so, he quickly picked out Gabriella. She was sitting with Taylor a few rows behind the team bench.

She saw him looking and waved, while Taylor shot him a thumbs-up. Troy waved back, glad that the whole Spirit-Ball-date fiasco hadn't kept Gabriella away from the game. He wished he could have talked to her about the whole dance mess, but after basketball practice yesterday his father had insisted on taking the whole family out for a pre-game dinner. By the time they got home it had been too late to call.

His smile faded as he noticed Sharpay sitting nearby. She was waving a huge sign that read GO WILDCATS! When she saw Troy looking, she jumped up and waved. Then she flipped her sign over. On the other side, in bright Wildcat red, were the words TROY RULES! Below that was a little drawing. Troy squinted at it, feeling his face turn red as he realized it was a picture of himself and Sharpay standing hand in hand. As if that weren't bad enough, both of them were wearing little gold crowns.

Troy shuddered. He had nothing against Sharpay, but he definitely wasn't looking forward to going to the dance with her. Especially when he really *should* be going with someone else . . .

"Come on, dude," Chad said, slapping him on the back and breaking him out of his thoughts. "Let's hit the showers. We need to get out of here and get ready for the dance."

Troy smiled weakly. A promise was a promise . . .

"You're on," he said. "So does this mean you and Taylor are back together again?"

"Sort of," Chad said. "Um, I guess. That is, I haven't really asked her." He shrugged. "But hey, I'm sure things will work out."

Troy couldn't help feeling a twinge of envy. How could Chad be so casual about something like that? But he pushed the thought aside. "Let's go," Troy said, leading the way towards the locker room.

Gabriella stared at herself in the full-length mirror on the bathroom door, smoothing her skirt. She was dressed in a pretty blue dress with a flowing skirt. Her dark hair was piled up loosely, allowing a few tendrils to fall in soft curls around her face. The only thing wrong with the picture was her expression. No matter what she did, she couldn't seem to muster a smile.

"Oh, honey! You look beautiful!"

Gabriella turned to see her mother standing in the hallway, her hands clasped in front of her and a proud smile on her face. For once, her mother had been home all day, though she'd been working at the computer for most of the time Gabriella had spent getting ready.

"Thanks." Gabriella tried to sound excited but failed miserably. Her voice came out in a sad croak.

Her mother immediately noticed her lack of enthusiasm. Her smile was replaced by a look of concern.

"What's wrong?" she asked. "Aren't you feeling well?" She hurried forward to put a hand to Gabriella's forehead.

Gabriella brushed her away. "It's nothing like that," she mumbled, feeling tears spring to her eyes. This whole time she'd been planning to wait until after Spirit Week to confront her mother about what she'd overheard – to face the truth. But suddenly she just couldn't stand it for another second. "I'm just upset because this could be my last dance ever at East High!"

Her mother looked confused. "What are you talking about?" she asked. "There will be lots of other dances."

"But not for me, right? Not here." Gabriella shook her head, trying desperately to contain her tears. "You don't have to keep it a secret any more, Mum. I heard you on the phone the other night. I know we're moving again."

"What?" This time her mother looked startled. "Moving? Where did you get that idea?"

"From you." Gabriella quickly told her about the phone call she'd overheard. "Sorry for eavesdropping – I didn't mean to. But I couldn't help it and then when I heard what you were talking about I–"

"Wait!" Her mother held up one hand. "You mean you heard me talking about going to New

York and thought we were *moving* there?" She laughed and put both hands to her cheeks.

Gabriella stared at her. "Why are you laughing? This isn't funny."

"I'm sorry, honey." Her mother swallowed another chuckle. "I don't mean to laugh; I can see that you're upset. But there's no reason to be – we're not going anywhere. It's just like I told you on your first day at East High. We're here until you graduate."

"But . . . but . . ." Gabriella blinked, trying to take in what her mother was saying. "Then why were you talking about notifying my school before you go to New York? And then a couple of days ago you were joking about designing Broadway outfits on the side, and so I just thought . . ."

Her mother stepped forward and put an arm around Gabriella's shoulders, giving her a hug. "I'm taking a business trip to New York City in a month or two," she explained. "And since I'll have a few free days while I'm there, I thought it would be fun if you came along." She smiled. "And it's true, I might have had Broadway on my mind lately – with your new interest in musical theatre, I thought we could try to see a couple of shows while we're there."

Gabriella just stared at her. Could it be true? "But you've been working so hard lately," she said. "All those late hours . . ."

"You're right, I have, and I'm sorry I haven't had more time to spend with you." Her mother shrugged. "I thought I told you, though – my company is in the middle of switching over to a new computer system."

Now that she mentioned it, that did sound vaguely familiar to Gabriella. But she still wasn't sure what it had to do with anything. "Um, so?"

"So we're all having to do twice as much work as usual just to keep up." Her mother gave her shoulders an extra squeeze. "That's why I told my boss I couldn't possibly do the New York trip until all that's settled."

"Oh." The pieces were falling into place. Now

that she knew the truth, Gabriella was starting to feel rather stupid. How could she have jumped to conclusions without taking a more careful look at all the facts? If she did that sort of thing in chemistry class, she would fail – if she didn't blow up the lab first.

Her mother smiled and stepped back, reaching out to adjust a strand of hair falling down into Gabriella's eyes. "So, are you ready to go enjoy your dance now?" she asked.

"Sure!" Gabriella smiled – and this time it took no effort at all. It felt as if a huge weight had been lifted off her shoulders. She couldn't wait to tell Kelsi the good news. Of course, she still wasn't sure what was going on with Troy . . .

But we'll work it out, she thought with a shiver of relief. *After all, we have plenty of time.*

CHAPTER TEN

"Smile, Troy. Everybody's looking at us." Sharpay patted her blonde hair, which was twisted up on top of her head in an elaborate style. "Of course, can you blame them? We look sensational. Talk about a power couple!"

Troy forced a weak smile. He was used to people staring at him when he played ball, but it definitely felt strange to walk into the dance with Sharpay clinging to his arm. His heart was thumping beneath his dark blazer and his palms felt sweaty.

What's my problem? he wondered. I've only walked into this gym a thousand times before.

But tonight felt different. Much different. And it was only partly because the East High gym didn't look anything like itself. The decorations committee had done a fantastic job, transforming it completely in the few hours since the game had finished. It was still decked out in Wildcat colours, but instead of team banners and retired jerseys, those colours came from balloons, painted backdrops and garlands of streamers. The place was already packed.

"Hey, Bolton! Nice shooting today!" somebody called from nearby.

Troy raised a hand in response, but Sharpay answered before he could say anything.

"Thank you, anonymous person," she called out. "Troy always enjoys comments from his fans."

"Knock it off, Sharpay," Troy muttered. "You're making me sound like a snob."

She raised one carefully groomed eyebrow. "Isn't that sweet," she said. "Our little superstar is a populist at heart." She shrugged. "You'll get over that after a while in the spotlight. Trust me."

Troy barely heard her. He'd glanced over his shoulder just in time to see Gabriella walking into the gym with Kelsi and Zeke. The three of them were all holding hands and giggling.

Troy's heart almost stopped. He had never seen Gabriella look quite so beautiful. As he watched, she threw her head back and laughed at something Zeke had just said, looking happy and excited. Then she waved to Taylor, who was hurrying towards her.

"Excuse me," Troy said to Sharpay. "I just need to go say hi to—"

But Sharpay had followed his gaze and spotted Gabriella herself. "Not so fast," she interrupted, yanking him back before he could get more than two steps away. "You're my date, remember? All mine." She smiled smugly. "That means you'd better stay put. Especially since it's almost time for Principal Matsui to crown the Spirit King and Queen."

"Oh, my gosh, you guys! The gym looks amazing!" Taylor exclaimed.

Gabriella smiled and glanced at Kelsi and Zeke. "Thanks," they all said in unison.

Taylor wrinkled her nose. "Too bad you couldn't do anything about the *smell.*"

Gabriella was about to answer that she didn't smell anything, but then she saw that Taylor was scowling at Chad, who was jogging towards them. He looked cute in a red tie and a coat that was a little too big for him. He traded an elaborate high-five greeting with Zeke, then turned to face Taylor.

"Hello," Taylor said, her voice cool. "Do I know you?"

"Look," Chad said, taking a step towards her. "Don't be like that, okay?"

Zeke rolled his eyes. "Later, dude," he said.

"I'd better go check on the cookies."

Chad was still staring at Taylor. "I already said I was sorry for goofing with you at the mall."

"Yeah." Taylor crossed her arms. "Easy to say that without all your friends watching."

Chad raised an eyebrow. "Is that what you're worried about?" he said. "You think I'm, like, embarrassed to be seen with you or something?"

"Maybe." Taylor shrugged. "Are you saying that's not it?"

"Maybe," Chad said.

Gabriella winced and exchanged a glance with Kelsi. Wrong thing to say, she thought. She could tell Chad was just joking around, as usual. But she could also tell that Taylor wasn't amused this time.

Taylor was glaring at Chad. "Then *maybe* you don't really want to be here with me after all," she said. She turned and started to walk away, chin in the air.

"Wait!" Chad sounded worried as he raced after her. "Hold on a second, okay? I was just goofing around, that's all. That's why I didn't say yes right away, too. I do want to be here with you – really! I swear!"

Taylor glanced over her shoulder at him. "Actions speak louder than words, Chad. Even *your* words – and they're pretty loud."

"Oh, yeah? Well, you just gave me the perfect idea about how to prove it to you." Chad cleared his throat, then grabbed Taylor's hand and held it up in the air. "Listen up, everyone!" he bellowed at the top of his lungs. "See this girl here? Me and her are here *together*, got that? And I'm proud of it! Hear me? *Proud, I say*!"

Gabriella giggled at the startled look on Taylor's face. People had turned to stare at them from all around, and a gaggle of cheerleaders standing nearby bent towards one another to whisper and laugh. Even Zeke had stopped halfway to the refreshments table to look back in shock.

Taylor's look of surprise was already turning to one of amusement. "Oh, Chad," she giggled, "you're such a weirdo. But I *might* forgive you if you get me a glass of punch."

Gabriella exchanged a smile with Kelsi as Taylor and Chad walked off together. She was glad to see that the two of them were back on track. Now if she could just straighten things out with Troy . . .

Before she could look for him, Principal Matsui stepped up onto a little platform beneath the home team basket and turned on his microphone. A whine of feedback got everyone's attention.

"Oh, good," Gabriella said. "He must be getting ready to announce the Spirit King and Queen. This should be fun."

Kelsi rolled her eyes. "Ooh, the suspense," she said sarcastically. "Everyone knows Troy and Sharpay are going to win."

"As you all know, the faculty and I have been watching you carefully all week to see which boy and girl we think showed the most school spirit during Spirit Week," Principal Matsui said. "I'm going to name our six finalists. Two of them will be our king and queen and the others will serve as their royal court. I'll call the finalists first in alphabetical order. Please come up here if your name is called." He cleared his throat and shuffled his notes. "Zeke Baylor!"

"Way to go, Zeke!" Chad howled, cupping both hands around his mouth.

Kelsi clapped. "That's so cool!" she cried. "You know, I never knew Zeke very well before. But he really does have a lot of school spirit."

"True," Gabriella said. "Plus he made that awesome play in the game today."

"Next," Principal Matsui continued, "I'd like to see Troy Bolton."

This time everyone cheered. Gabriella craned her neck to get a better look as Troy made his way towards the Principal. He was grinning bashfully and looking handsome in his jacket and tie.

"Now, can I see Ryan Evans?" Principal Matsui called next. "And Sharpay Evans."

"He might as well stop right there," Kelsi

said, clapping politely along with everyone else.

"Oh, come on," Gabriella said with a laugh. "Don't try to cheat a couple of cheerleaders out of their big mo–"

"Gabriella Montez," Principal Matsui called.

"What?" Gabriella squeaked, startled.

"Go up there!" Kelsi said, grinning and giving her a shove.

"And Kelsi Nielsen," the Principal finished. "Come on up!"

This time Gabriella was the one to grin. She grabbed Kelsi by the hand. "Come on," she said. "Our royal subjects await."

She couldn't help feeling bashful as she dragged Kelsi forward. It still felt a little strange to know that all eyes were on her. But starring in the winter musical had helped her to get over some of her stage fright. She even managed to wave a little as she made her way through the crowd to take her place with the others.

"Congrats," Troy whispered, leaning closer to her and smiling.

"You too," she said, suddenly feeling shy. "Listen, Troy. I'm sorry I didn't–"

"Don't worry about it," he whispered back. "I'm sorry I – you know." He tilted his head towards Sharpay. "I'll explain later."

"Me too." Gabriella smiled at him, knowing without a doubt that things would be back to normal between them very soon. "As soon as this king-and-queen thing is over, we can talk."

"Hush!" Sharpay hissed at both of them. "He's about to announce my – I mean, announce the winners' names."

Sure enough, Principal Matsui was shuffling his papers again. "Without further ado," he said into the microphone, "I give you your Spirit King and Queen – Zeke Baylor and Kelsi Nielsen!"

"What?" Zeke exclaimed, looking surprised.

"What?" Kelsi cried, looking stunned.

"What?" Sharpay squawked loudly, looking horrified. "You're kidding, right? Her? But she's – she's . . ." She seemed to run out of words as she stared at Kelsi. "She's not even wearing Wildcat colours!" she spluttered at last, pointing dramatically at Kelsi's green dress.

Principal Matsui looked confused. "I'm sorry, Sharpay," he said. "That really wasn't a requirement."

"Ooh!" This time Sharpay didn't even try. Throwing both hands over her head, she stomped off.

"Sharpay, wait!" Ryan called, charging off after her.

The Principal shrugged, then spoke into the microphone again. "Congratulations to Zeke and Kelsi," he said. "Both of them showed true school spirit by working tirelessly this week to make this dance happen. So let's see them enjoy it – get out there and dance, you two!"

Zeke had recovered from his surprise by now and appeared to be enjoying himself as he waved to the crowd. Then he turned to Kelsi, who still hadn't moved.

"May I, Your Majesty?" he said, holding out a

hand as the DJ started a song.

"Go on!" Gabriella whispered with a grin, shoving Kelsi towards him.

A moment later, the two of them were swaying awkwardly to the music. Zeke kept looking around and grinning uncertainly, while Kelsi kept her eyes on her own feet.

"They don't look too happy to be out there dancing in front of everyone, do they?" Troy commented to Gabriella.

"Not really." She shot him a sidelong glance. "Maybe we should get out there and help them out?"

He grinned and took her by the hand. "I thought you'd never ask."

Something new is on the way!

Look for the next book in the Disney High School Musical: Stories from East High series. . .

POETRY IN MOTION

By Alice Alfonsi

Based on the Disney Channel Original Movie *High School Musical*, written by Peter Barsocchini

Troy Bolton stifled a yawn. At the front of the room, Ms Barrington was reading yet another Scottish ode.

English was Troy's first class after lunch. Today he'd downed two cartons of milk and a turkey sandwich – good choices for athletic nutrition, but a seriously bad combo for listening to 200-year-old poetry.

Pinching the back of his hand, Troy tried to

stay alert. But his eyelids felt as if they'd been loaded down with free weights. His head dropped once, twice, three times. Then *bop*! A little paper aeroplane hit him. Troy sat up straight. He was definitely awake now.

The tiny projectile had dropped onto his desk. He picked it up and unfolded the paper. Right away, he recognized the neat, delicate handwriting . . .

O stay awake, Troy Bolton!
Push your comprehension,
'cause if you nod off one more time,
you'll be napping in detention!

Poetically yours,
Gabriella

Before he could stop himself, Troy laughed out loud.

At the front of the room, the teacher looked up from her textbook. "Is something *funny*, Mr Bolton?"

"No, Ms Barrington," Troy said. He quickly crumpled the note, hiding it in his fist.

The tall, slender teacher peered at him through her black, oval-shaped glasses. Ms Barrington wasn't very old, but her floor-length skirts, severely upswept red hair and love of 18th-century poetry made her seem ancient to Troy.

"It certainly *sounds* as though you found something amusing in Robert Burns' poem," she said. "Why don't you share it with us?"

Troy silently groaned. Gabriella Montez was sitting in the next row. She'd been smiling at him when he read her funny note. Now that it had triggered trouble, she looked really upset.

Sorry, she silently mouthed to Troy.

It's okay, he mouthed back.

Ms Barrington tapped her foot. "Mr Bolton? I'm waiting." She glanced at Gabriella and narrowed her eyes. "Enlighten us all with your reaction to this poet's words. What exactly made you laugh?"

"Umm . . ." Troy swallowed. He felt heat rising in his cheeks.

Gabriella was about to speak up when a voice came from across the room.

"My man wasn't laughing," Chad Danforth insisted.

Ms Barrington put a hand on her hip and turned her head. Now she had a new target. "Is that right, Mr Danforth?"

Troy froze. Chad was one of his best friends. He always watched Troy's back, especially on the basketball court. But now was not the time for his team-mate to cover for him!

"Straight up," Chad said. "You misheard Troy. He was just clearing his throat."

Ms Barrington narrowed her gaze. "I misheard him?"

"Sure," Chad said. "I mean, what dude in his right mind would laugh at what you just read?"

Troy cringed. "Uh, right. Sorry to interrupt, Ms Barrington. I just had to, you know, clear my dry throat. Like Chad said."

"You see how powerful that poem was?" Chad went on. "Like subliminal advertising or something."

"All right, Chad. That's enough." Ms Barrington cleared her own throat. "Let's move on, shall we?"

"Okay by me," Chad mumbled, exchanging a glance with his team-mates in the last row. Two points, he silently mouthed to them.

Zeke Baylor and Jason Cross quietly sniggered and Troy exhaled with relief. He had no doubt that Chad had just saved him and Gabriella from all the joys of detention.

At the front of the room, Ms Barrington lifted her chin and addressed the class. "For the last four weeks, you've all been studying a number of poets. Now it's time to test what you've absorbed."

She snapped her textbook shut and leaned back against the edge of her desk. "But I'm not going to give you a traditional multiple-choice quiz. In my view, that's not the way to test whether you've really learned what poetry is all about. Next Tuesday, at a special school assembly, each of you will read an original poem. This assignment will be a very important part of your semester grade. But I'm sure each of you will rise to the occasion."

Chad scratched his head of floppy brown hair. "Excuse me, Ms Barrington?" He waved his hand. "What do you mean, each of us will 'read an original poem'?"

The English teacher frowned. "What's not to understand, Chad? You will write a poem. Then you will read the poem you wrote. Simple."

"But . . ." Chad blinked. "In front of the whole school?"

"Yes, in front of the whole school. As I said, it's a very special assembly." Ms Barrington clapped her hands.

"So, will you accept poems written in any style?" Taylor asked, turning to a fresh page in her notebook. "Or just the Romantic style?" She lifted her pen, ready to scribble a detailed answer.

"Any style of poetry is welcome," Ms Barrington said. "We've covered a number of them in class, but I've given you all a reading list. Inspiration abounds! Take advantage of it."

Kelsi's hand went up again. She nervously pushed up her round glasses.

"Ms Barrington?" she asked, her small voice barely rising above the brim of her cap. "You're not really going to make it mandatory that we read our own poems, are you?"

"Of course!" Ms Barrington boomed. "Reading your own poetry is a vital experience and an essential part of the assignment."

Now Sharpay Evans raised her hand.

"I, for one, think it's a brilliant assignment!" she said. "Thank you, Ms Barrington, for giving us this opportunity to spotlight our individual talents!"

Ms Barrington nodded. "You're welcome, Sharpay."

Troy noticed Taylor rolling her eyes. Gabriella just sighed. Then the bell rang and everyone scattered.

"Dude, I owe you," Troy said, walking up to Chad a few minutes later. "Thanks for the save back there."

"No problem." Chad said. "Just pay me back with some sweet passes on the court."

"You got it," Troy smiled and the two sealed the deal by knocking fists.

Taylor McKessie tossed Chad a warm smile as she walked into the hallway. "Easy assignment, huh, Chad?" she called.

"The assignment?" Chad said, automatically tensing. "Uh . . . sure . . . piece o' cake," he told her, forcing a smile and trying to seem relaxed.

The moment Taylor was gone, he grimaced. "As if I'm going to do it," he whispered to Troy. "Yeah, right."

Troy blinked. "What do you mean?"

"I'm not doing that poetry assignment," Chad said. "That's what I mean."

Troy couldn't believe what he was hearing. "Chad, you have to. You heard Ms Barrington. It's a big part of your semester grade."

Chad waved his hand. "I'll tell her I've got writer's block or something. She'll let me off the hook. But I am *not* getting up on East's school hall stage, in front of the entire school, spouting rhymes about rainbows and red, red roses. This whole poetry thing freaks me out!"

"Freaks you out?" Sharpay piped up, overhearing him. She tossed her blonde hair and threw a special grin Troy's way. "What's the biggie, guys? Roses are red, violets are blue. The *writing* is simple. What's key is the *presentation.* Just find the right costume, practise in front of a mirror and you'll do fine!"

Chad looked horrified.

Sharpay didn't notice. She checked her watch. "Sorry, I've got to run," she chirped, dashing off. "Drama class next, and I haven't warmed my vocal chords! Buh-bye!"

Chad shuddered. He turned to Troy. "Did you hear what she said?" he whispered. "A *costume*?"

"Oh, wow. That's right. I forgot." Troy

smacked his forehead, suddenly remembering. "Your leotard incident."

"Dude, don't even go there." Chad shook his head, looking sick to his stomach. He glanced around, making sure no one was close enough to hear.

Troy didn't blame him. When they were in fourth grade, their teacher had convinced Chad to recite a poem at the Albuquerque Renaissance Fair. Unfortunately, she'd failed to warn him that he'd have to wear Elizabethan tights, silk bloomers and a hat with a feather.

All the boys in their class were laughing hysterically at him the second he stepped onto the stage. Chad had memorized the love poem perfectly. He was actually hoping to impress a girl named Rhonda. But when he saw every boy in his class laughing in the front row, he forgot the lines and began to stammer. Then he dropped his hat, bent over to pick it up and his bloomers split open.

It hadn't been a good day.

Six months later, Rhonda moved to Denver. But Chad never forgot the look on her face as he ran off the stage, mortified.

"I can't do it, man," Chad whispered. "I just can't."

"But–"

"Sorry." Chad shook his head. "I'll catch you later!"

Troy stood like a statue in the hallway. A couple of kids bumped into him. He didn't notice. He was too upset by what Chad intended to do – and not to do.

Troy doubted very much whether Ms Barrington was going to let anyone off the hook for this assignment. Their English teacher was really tough. She'd never accept an excuse of 'writer's block'.

HIGH SCHOOL MUSICAL

Book of the Film

Adapted by N.B. Grace

Based on the Disney Channel Original Movie "High School Musical", written by Peter Barsocchini

Parragon

Bath · New York · Singapore · Hong Kong · Cologne · Delhi · Melbourne

This is a Parragon book

First published in 2006
Parragon
Queen Street House
4 Queen Street
Bath, BA1 1HE, UK

ISBN 978-1-4054-9149-5
Printed in China

HIGH SCHOOL MUSICAL

CHAPTER ONE

It was a magical New Year's Eve at a vacation resort in the mountains. Gleaming white snow covered the ground, stars sparkled in the crisp, clear air, and everyone was beginning to get in the party mood.

Everyone, that is, except Troy Bolton and his father, Jack, who were still on the basketball court, playing one-on-one. They were covered with sweat, but they were having too much fun to stop.

Troy had the ball, and he was doing a good job of getting around his dad. After all, Troy was on the high school basketball team. Not only that, he was the team captain. He had the smooth moves and explosive action of a real star.

But Jack was more than just Troy's dad. Jack was also the basketball team's coach. So Mr. Bolton gave his son advice as they played.

"Keep working left, Troy," Mr. Bolton said. "The guy guarding you in the championship game won't expect that. You'll torch him."

Troy nodded, breathing hard. "By going left -" he said.

"He'll look middle, you take it downtown," his dad - and coach - explained.

Troy nodded again. "Like this?"

He spun past his father, jumped, and sunk a reverse layup. The ball whistled cleanly through the basket. Nothing but net!

His father grinned. "Sweet."

Troy grinned back. Nothing felt better than playing basketball when you were in the groove!

They could have played all night, but just then Troy's mum walked into the gym. She was wearing a sequined party dress and clearly had things other than B-ball on her mind.

"Boys? Hello?" she called. Once she got their attention, she went on. "Did we really fly all this way to play more basketball?"

Troy and his father glanced at each other slyly. They knew she didn't really want an answer to that question, but they gave her one anyway. In perfect unison, they shrugged and said, "Yeah."

Mrs. Bolton gave an exasperated sigh. "It's the last night of vacation. The party . . . ? Remember?"

Actually, they had both totally forgotten the big New Year's Eve party that the resort was holding, but they knew it wasn't wise to admit that.

"Oh, right, right," Mr. Bolton said quickly. "New Year's Eve." He hesitated, then asked, with some fear, "Do we have to wear funny hats?"

"Absolutely," she said firmly. "And we're due

in half an hour. Troy, they have a kids' party downstairs in the Freestyle Club."

"Kids' party?" Troy protested. That made him sound like a toddler!

"Young adults," his mum quickly amended. "Now go shower up."

With heavy sighs, Troy and his father did as she said.

As Troy took one last glance at the basketball court, he thought, The championship game is in a couple of weeks! I should be practising, not going to some stupid "kids' party"! Besides, how much fun could hanging out with a bunch of kids possibly be. . . .

Meanwhile, in another part of the lodge, another mother was about to tear her daughter away from a different fascinating activity.

Gabriella Montez was comfortably curled up in an overstuffed chair in the sitting area. She was enjoying the peace and quiet - everyone else was already at the party - and had totally lost herself in a book called *If You Only Knew Me*. It was the best book she had read since, well, since the last book she checked out of the library, and she couldn't wait to get to the end.

However, she didn't even get to the next page. The book was lifted right out of her hands, and she looked up to see her mother standing over her.

"Gabby, it's New Year's Eve," Mrs. Montez said. "Enough reading."

"But, Mum, I'm almost done and - " Gabriella protested.

Her mother just shook her head. "There's a teen party," she said firmly. "I've laid out your best dress. Go."

Gabriella eyed her mother's sparkly party dress and sighed. She knew when she was defeated.

She nodded, but asked, "Can I have my book back?"

Her mother handed it over and Gabriella headed toward her room to change. As soon as she was out of her mum's sight, however, she opened the book and began reading as she walked.

She might have to go to some stupid teen party, she thought, but she didn't plan to turn her brain off until the very last minute.

A short time later, Troy and Gabriella were in the teen club, feeling out of place. It was packed with kids wearing goofy party hats, blowing on noisemakers, and laughing.

Everyone else seems to be having fun, Troy thought glumly. He had showered and dressed in nice trousers and an ironed shirt, but he just wished he was back on the basketball court.

In another part of the room, Gabriella sat by herself, wearing the dress her mum had laid out. I could be back in my room, reading, Gabriella thought wistfully. I was just getting to the good part, too.

Neither one of them was having any fun at all.

Most of the kids in the room were watching a karaoke contest that was in full swing on a raised stage. As two teenagers finished their song, the MC called out cheerfully, "How about that for a couple of snowboarders?!"

The audience applauded, and the MC started looking around the room, trying to spot anyone else who was willing to sing karaoke to a room full of strangers. Spotlights swirled over the crowd, and the music played even louder to get the partygoers' adrenaline pumping.

"All right," the MC said into his mic. "Let's see who is gonna rock the house next. . . ."

That was the cue. The music stopped. The two spotlights picked out the next karaoke "volunteers."

One spotlight was on Troy.

The other was on Gabriella.

Both looked startled, and even a little terrified. They shook their heads, but it was no use. The MC jumped into the crowd and pulled them up onto the stage.

Troy and Gabriella were mortified. Somehow - they weren't quite sure how it happened -

microphones were put in their hands. There they were, stuck. Onstage. The centre of attention. And no way to escape.

Before either one of them could actually faint or throw up from fear, the music started.

Well, here goes, Troy thought with resignation. Might as well make the best of it . . .

He started singing, softly and carefully. He could barely get the words out. It was all he could do to read the lyrics on the screen of the karaoke machine and try to stay in tune. He sang:

"Livin' in my own world
Didn't understand
That anything can happen
When you take a chance"

No one seemed to be paying much attention to them. That was a *good* thing, Gabriella thought. And, after all, if this boy was willing to risk public humiliation, she might as well be a good sport and try to sing, too.

She opened her mouth and began singing. Although her voice was just above a whisper, it was sweet and pure. She sang:

"I never believed in
What I couldn't see
I never opened my heart
To all the possibilities"

All right, she thought. I can do this. It's not too terrible.

Okay, Troy thought. At least people aren't throwing things at us.

Still, they were too nervous to really belt out the song. They kept singing though, alternating the lines of the ballad.

Finally, they looked at each other, hoping for a little help from their partner in embarrassment. As they really saw each other, they both experienced something they never had before.

Troy felt a spark of electricity run over his skin. Gabriella felt a warm glow flood through her body. They smiled and, for the first time, began singing to each other. They sang more loudly, more boldly, with more self-assurance.

Suddenly, everyone in the room started to notice: there was something special going on up onstage! Kids began crowding around the edge of the stage, listening and swaying to the music. And now Troy and Gabriella were starting to enjoy themselves. Their nervousness was forgotten as they smiled into each other's eyes.

Before long, they were dancing across the stage and back again, as confident as if they were performing at an arena. As they moved to the music, they never took their eyes off each other.

When the song was over, the crowd applauded and cheered. Troy and Gabriella smiled, breathless and a little stunned by what had just happened.

Troy leaned over and said, "I'm Troy."

Gabriella nodded. "Gabriella."

Neither one of them could stop smiling. Both of them felt an excited, fizzy feeling inside, as if the world had just become a lot more fun.

CHAPTER TWO

They were still giddy from the excitement of their impromptu performance, so they went for a walk outside in the cold, sparkling air.

"You have an awesome voice," Troy said. "You're a singer, right?"

Gabriella shrugged. "Just the church choir is all." She smiled and admitted, "I tried to do a solo and nearly fainted."

"Why's that?" he asked, surprised.

She shook her head at the memory. "I took

one look at all the people staring only at me, and the next thing I knew, I was staring at the ceiling. End of solo career."

"The way you sang just now, that's hard to believe," he said sincerely.

"This is the first time I've done something like this," she answered.

Troy knew how she felt. "Completely," he agreed.

"You sound like you've done a lot of singing, too," she said.

"Oh, sure, lots," he said jokingly. "My showerhead is very impressed with me."

At that moment, everyone around them started chanting in unison: "Ten! Nine! Eight! . . ."

The New Year's Eve countdown had begun.

Troy and Gabriella glanced at each other, then just as quickly looked away.

"Seven! Six! Five! Four! . . ."

This was a magical night, Gabriella thought, wishing it would last longer.

I can't believe I didn't want to come to this party! Troy thought. *This was awesome!*

"Three! Two! One!"

Everyone began cheering and blowing on their noisemakers. Fireworks burst in the sky in showers of red, gold, and blue. Everyone was celebrating - but Troy and Gabriella were suddenly feeling awkward.

People kiss each other on New Year's Eve, Troy thought. *Should I - ?*

It's a tradition to kiss when the clock strikes midnight, Gabriella thought. *Will he - ?*

Neither one moved. After a few seconds, she smiled and said, "I guess I'd better go find my mum and wish her Happy New Year."

Troy nodded. The spell was broken, and he was a little relieved. "Me, too," he said. "I mean, not *your* mum - my mum . . . and dad. I'll call you tomorrow."

He pulled out his mobile, quickly snapped a picture of her, then handed her the phone.

"Put your number in."

Gabriella grabbed her own phone and handed it to him. "You, too - "

They quickly switched phones and tapped in their numbers. Then Gabriella turned to leave. Troy stopped her.

"Singing with you was the most fun I've had this vacation," he said sincerely. "Where do you - "

Another series of fireworks exploded overhead, drowning out whatever he was saying.

Gabriella was already at the stairs. She waved back, smiling, then vanished. Troy stood absolutely still, gazing after her.

A week later, school had started again at East High School in Albuquerque, New Mexico. It was the first morning back after winter vacation, and the scene was bedlam. Kids were piling out of buses, yelling at each other, showing off new clothes.

As Troy entered the courtyard, under the banner that read "Happy New Year, Wildcats," other students gave him high fives, low fives, and side fives.

His friend and basketball teammate Chad came up to him, yelling, "Yo, doggie! Troy, my hoops boy!"

Chad had wild, curly hair and a wired attitude to match. He was the loyal number two to Troy's number one and, before Troy could blink, he found that Chad had drawn in all the other members of the team. They were happy to see him, excited to be back together, and totally keyed up about the championship game, now just a couple of weeks away.

"Hey, Chad," Troy said. He waved at the other players. "Dudes . . . Happy New Year."

"Oh, yes, it will be a Happy Wildcat New Year," Chad shouted. "Because in two weeks we are going to the championships, with *you* leading us to infinity and beyond!"

Troy laughed, and the other members of the Wildcat basketball team nodded and high-fived each other. Chad was right. They were about to fulfill their destiny!

At that moment, Sharpay and Ryan Evans

pushed their way through the basketball posse. Both of them tossed their hair as only copresidents of the Drama Club could.

As usual, Sharpay looked Barbie-doll perfect, with blown-out hair, full makeup, and fashionable clothes. Her brother, Ryan, looked just as hip.

Zeke, one of the basketball players, watched Sharpay as she haughtily pushed her way through the crowd. "Hey, the ice princess has returned from the North Pole," he muttered to his crew.

"Yeah, she probably spent the holidays the way she always does," Chad said.

Jason, another basketball player, willingly filled the role of straight man. "How's that?" he asked.

"Shopping for mirrors!" Chad cracked.

He howled like a wolf in appreciation of his own joke. His teammates joined in.

Still howling, they walked by Taylor McKessie, the president of the Chemistry Club, who was accompanied by a few of her brainiac friends.

Taylor scornfully eyeballed the basketball players, then said to her friends, "Ah, behold the zoo animals heralding the new year. How tribal."

As her friends haughtily agreed, the bell rang and everybody hurried to their homerooms.

The crowds had thinned somewhat as Principal Matsui walked down the hall, escorting a new student. It was a nervous Gabriella and her mother, who were trying to listen as the principal gave them his sales pitch.

"We're consistently rated in the top ten academically in the state, and I think you'll also find this a wonderful community atmosphere," Principal Matsui said.

Gabriella tried to smile as she peeked in a window in a classroom door. The scene inside was total, first-day-back-at-school chaos. Her stomach flipped over and she cast an appealing look at her mother.

"Mum, my stomach – "

" – is always nervous on the first day at a new

school," her mother finished reassuringly. "You'll do great, you always do. And I've made my company promise that I can't be transferred again until you graduate."

Gabriella smiled weakly. This was always the worst part, she reminded herself.

"Worry not, Gabriella," Principal Matsui said. "I've reviewed your impressive transcripts. I expect your light will shine very brightly here at East High."

Gabriella knew he was trying to be helpful, but her stomach twisted even more at these words. "I don't want to be the school freaky genius girl again," she whispered to her mum.

Mrs. Montez hugged her. "Just be Gabriella," she said warmly.

Gabriella went to her homeroom with Ms. Darbus, the school's drama teacher. True to her theatrical background, she was flamboyantly dressed in a long, flowing dress and wore oversized glasses.

Gabriella quickly took her seat, doing her best

to be invisible. She didn't see Troy enter with his best bud, Chad - but as Troy said hello to other students, he caught a glimpse of her from the corner of his eye.

Surprised, he craned his neck for a better look, but other students kept getting in the way. That girl, he thought. She looked just like - but what would the girl from New Year's Eve be doing here. . . ?

Before he could get a better look, the final bell rang and everybody scrambled to sit at their desks.

Ms. Darbus stood in front of the class as if she were taking centre stage in a Broadway theatre. "I trust you all had splendid holidays," she said. "Check the sign-up sheets in the lobby for new activities, especially our winter musical. There'll be single auditions for the supporting roles, as well as pairs auditions for our two leads - "

Chad looked around at his basketball team-mates, grinned, and blew a raspberry at the mention of the musical.

Ms. Darbus glared at him. "Mr. Danforth, this is a place of learning, not a hockey arena," she snapped.

Troy was still craning his neck, trying to see the new girl who looked so much like Gabriella. Finally, frustrated, he pulled his mobile from his pocket and thumbed through the menu.

The photo of Gabriella that he took on New Year's Eve popped up on the screen. He stared at it, remembering that magical night, as Ms. Darbus happily burbled on.

"There is also a final sign-up for next week's Scholastic Decathlon Competition," she said. "Chem Club president Taylor McKessie can answer your questions on that."

Meanwhile, Troy hit the SEND button on his phone. Suddenly, Gabriella's phone started ringing wildly. At first, she didn't even react. After all, who would be calling her?

Sharpay and Ryan grabbed for their phones. After all, wouldn't *every* call be for them?

Ms. Darbus strode to the front of the room,

the light of battle in her eyes. "Ah, the cell phone menace returns to our crucible of learning!" she cried. She grabbed a plastic bucket labelled "Cell-itary Confinement" and held it out to the brother and sister. "Sharpay and Ryan, your phones please, and I'll see you in detention."

They rolled their eyes, but deposited their phones in the bucket. The ringing, however, went on.

Ms. Darbus's gaze swept the room, searching for the source of the nefarious ring. Blushing, Gabriella fumbled in her backpack. As she finally dug her phone out and started to turn it off, she saw . . . Troy Bolton's photo?

Her eyes widened with surprise and she accidentally hit ANSWER instead of END.

Now Troy was staring in surprise at his phone, where he saw Gabriella's photo. But Ms. Darbus was looming over Gabriella and holding out her plastic bucket.

"We have zero tolerance on cell phones during

class," the drama teacher said sternly. "So, we'll get to know each other at detention. Phone, please . . . and welcome to East High, Miss Montez."

As she walked back to the front of the class, she saw Troy holding his phone and held out her bucket. "Mr. Bolton, I see your phone is involved. Splendid, we'll see you in detention, as well."

Troy sighed and dropped his phone in the bucket.

Behind him, Chad protested. "That's not even a possibility, Ms. Darbus, your honour, because we have basketball practice and Troy is – "

Ms. Darbus whirled around and glared at him. "That's fifteen minutes for you, too, Mr. Danforth. Count 'em!"

At the back of the class, Taylor smirked and whispered to one of her brainiac friends, "That could be tough for Chad, since he probably can't count that high."

She should have known better. Ms. Darbus had better hearing than a bat.

"Taylor McKessie," she said sharply. "Fifteen minutes."

Taylor's jaw dropped. She had never had to serve a minute of detention in her entire life!

But it was no use protesting. Ms. Darbus had already whirled around to survey the rest of the class. "Shall the carnage continue? Vacation is over, people. Way over! Any more comments? Questions?"

Jason, one of the basketball players, thought it was about time to restore a good mood to this morning's homeroom. He raised his hand and asked sincerely, "So how were your holidays, Ms. Darbus?"

As everyone looked at him in disbelief, the bell rang. The class bolted for the door, relieved to be free of Darbus rule for the time being.

CHAPTER THREE

Troy waited anxiously in the hall outside Ms. Darbus's homeroom, hanging back as his friends went on to their next classes.

Finally, Gabriella came out, and he walked towards her, hardly able to breathe.

When Gabriella saw him, her eyes widened in disbelief.

She said, "I don't - "

" - believe it," Troy finished in a whisper.

Gabriella nodded. "Me - "

" – either," Troy finished again. "But how . . ."

"My mum's company transferred her here to Albuquerque," Gabriella explained. She shook her head in disbelief. "I can't believe you live here. I looked for you at the lodge on New Year's Day, but – "

"We had to leave first thing," Troy said, still whispering.

Gabriella looked puzzled. "Why are you whispering?"

He looked a little embarrassed. "Oh, well, my friends know I went snowboarding, but I didn't tell them about the . . . singing . . . thing."

"Too much for them to handle?" she asked knowingly.

"It was . . . cool," Troy said quickly. He didn't want her getting the idea that he hadn't liked their singing debut! "But, my friends – that's not what I do. That was like a . . . different person."

They had reached the lobby, where activity

sign-up sheets were posted. Troy pointed at the sheet for the winter musical auditions.

"Now that you've met Ms. Darbus, I'll bet you can't wait to sign up for that," he said grinning.

Gabriella laughed. "I won't be signing up for *anything* here for a while," she said. "I just want to get to know the school." She glanced at him shyly. "But if you signed up, I'd consider coming to the show."

Troy shook his head. He couldn't even imagine the reaction he'd get if he signed up for the high school musical! "That's completely impossible," he said.

From behind him, Sharpay's voice said sweetly, "What's impossible, Troy? I wouldn't think 'impossible' is even in your vocabulary." As they turned to look at Sharpay, she gestured toward Gabriella. "So nice of you to show our new classmate around."

She raised one eyebrow as she saw Gabriella looking at the musical sign-up sheet. Very deliberately, Sharpay stepped in front of

Gabriella and signed her name with a flourish.

In fact, Gabriella noticed, Sharpay's signature took up the entire sign-up sheet!

But Sharpay looked at her, the picture of innocence, and said, "Oh . . . were you going to sign up, too? My brother and I have starred in all of the school's productions, and we really welcome newcomers." She smiled, ever so sweetly, then added, "There are a lot of supporting roles in this show. I'm sure we could find something for you."

"No, no," Gabriella said hastily. "I was just looking over the bulletin board. Lots going on at this school. Wow." I'm babbling, she thought. I have to stop it! Now! She pointed to Sharpay's huge signature. "Nice penmanship," she added weakly, before hurrying away to her next class.

Now that Sharpay had been left alone with Troy, she decided to seize the opportunity. "So, Troy," she said coyly, "I missed you during vacation. What'd you do?"

He shrugged. "Practised basketball. Snowboarding. More basketball."

Sharpay nodded cheerfully and, using all of her dramatic training to sound as if she really cared, asked, "When's the big game?"

"Two weeks." Troy sounded resolute, determined. Two weeks until we're either champions - or we're not, he thought.

"You're so dedicated," Sharpay said, batting her eyelashes just a bit. After a moment, she added, "Just like me. I hope you'll come watch me in the musical? Promise?"

Just like Sharpay to bring the conversation back to herself, Troy thought wryly. But he smiled and nodded as he walked away.

A few hours later, Troy and the basketball team had gathered in the gym for practice. Troy and Chad challenged each other by running a pressure drill, while the other boys ran a weave drill.

"Hey, you know that school-musical thing?"

Troy asked as he tried to get around Chad. "Is it true you get extra credit just for auditioning?"

"Who cares?" Chad asked as he blocked Troy.

Troy raised one eyebrow and tried to scoot around Chad from the other side. "It's good to get extra credit . . . for college and all," he said, trying to sound casual.

Chad laughed and shook his head. "Do you think LeBron James or Shaquille O'Neal ever auditioned for their school musical?" he asked mockingly.

"Maybe . . ." Troy said hesitantly.

"Troy, the music in those shows isn't hip-hop or rock or anything essential to the culture," Chad explained patiently. "It's like . . . *show music.* Costumes, makeup." He shuddered. "Frightening."

Troy shrugged, still trying to sound like it was no big deal. "I thought it might be a good laugh. Sharpay is kind of cute, too."

Now Chad looked at him with total disbelief. "So is a mountain lion, but you don't pet them."

Troy nodded, and gave up for the moment. Time to take charge of this practice, he thought. Time to focus. The championship game, he reminded himself sternly, is only weeks away.

He turned to his team. "All right, let's kick it in, run the shuffle drill," he yelled.

The team quickly took their positions and began bouncing basketballs and weaving around one another with the ease developed through hours of practise.

The balls began to bounce and the players began to move across the floor with a rhythmic, percussive movement. And Troy began to call out the practise drills.

"Coach said to
Fake right
And break left
Watch out for the pick
And keep an eye on defense
You gotta run the give and go
And take the ball to the hole

But don't be afraid
To shoot the outside 'J' "

The Wildcats had developed a team motto, and now Troy shouted it out to get his boys pumped up:

"Just keep ya' head in the game
Keep ya' head in the game
Just keep ya' head in the game
Don't be afraid to shoot the outside 'J' "

The team members smiled and moved even faster, smoother, better. Troy was a great captain, and he could motivate them like no one else!

Troy grabbed a ball and joined the drills, dribbling left around one player and right around another, still calling out drills.

When practice ended, everyone took deep breaths, smiling at how great they felt and how great they had looked. The Wildcats were definitely good to go for the championship!

CHAPTER FOUR

The next morning, Gabriella sat at a station in the chemistry lab, across the table from Taylor and next to Sharpay. The students were wearing neat white lab coats and busily setting up equipment as the chemistry teacher wrote equations on the blackboard.

Sharpay gave Gabriella a fake smile. Ever so casually, she said, "So, it seemed like you knew Troy Bolton."

Gabriella glanced up briefly, but she was

distracted by the teacher, who was solving the equation on the board. "Not really . . . I just asked him for directions," she said, even as she started checking the teacher's work on her scratch pad.

Sharpay raised the wattage of her smile just a bit. "Troy usually doesn't . . . interact . . . with new students."

"Why not?" Gabriella asked, not really listening. She looked at her equation. Hmmm. Her calculation was quite different from the teacher's. Should she say something? Maybe not. People didn't like it when you pointed out their mistakes. . . .

"It's pretty much basketball 24/7 with him," Sharpay said with a little laugh.

Now Gabriella wasn't listening to Sharpay at all. She rechecked her own calculation and murmured, "Pi to the eleventh power."

She thought she had said it quietly, but apparently not quietly enough.

The chemistry teacher turned around. "Yes, Miss Montez?"

"Oh, I'm sorry," Gabriella said, flustered. "I was just - "

Before she could finish her sentence, the teacher was standing by her chair, looking down at her notebook.

"Pi to the eleventh power?" the teacher said in surprise. "That's quite impossible." Then she whipped out a calculator and started punching in numbers. Across the table, Taylor had her calculator out as well, and was matching the teacher, keystroke for keystroke.

There was a brief, stunned pause. Then the teacher said, "I stand corrected." She turned back to the blackboard to revise her work. Then she looked over her shoulder, smiled warmly at Gabriella, and added, "And welcome aboard."

Gabriella blushed as Taylor stared at her, impressed.

Troy was strolling through the lobby on the way to his next class, when he caught sight of the musical audition sign-up sheet. His steps slowed.

It was crazy, he *knew* it was crazy, but he couldn't seem to stop thinking about the musical. He stood still, almost hypnotized by the piece of paper. He was so lost in his thoughts that he didn't notice Sharpay's brother, Ryan, who was hanging out nearby with a couple of the Drama Club kids.

Ryan's eyes narrowed suspiciously. When Troy finally moved on, Ryan ran up to the sheet, just to make sure. . . .

At that moment, Sharpay arrived. Ryan rushed up to her, breathless. "Troy Bolton was looking at our audition list!" he reported.

Sharpay stiffened, all senses suddenly alert. "Again? He was hanging around with that new girl, and they were both looking at the list." She paused a moment to think. "There's something freaky about her," Sharpay decided. "Where did she say she was from?"

Minutes later, Sharpay and Ryan were in the school library, doing an Internet search on

Gabriella. A number of newspaper articles immediately popped up on the screen.

"Whiz Kid Leads School to Scholastic Championship," read one headline.

"Sun High Marvel Aces Statewide Chemistry Competition," another headline said.

A photo of Gabriella showed her beaming into the camera and holding a number of awards.

As Sharpay printed out the article, Ryan said, "Whoa . . . an Einstein-ette. So why is she interested in our musical?"

"I'm not sure that she is," Sharpay said. "And we needn't concern ourselves with amateurs." She neatly folded the printouts and stood up. "*But* there's no harm in making certain that Gabriella is welcomed into school activities that are . . . appropriate . . . for her. After all, she loves pi."

And Ryan, who was always at least one step behind Sharpay, saw his sister's smile and knew that she had a plan.

* * *

Later that day, everyone who had been given detention had to serve their time.

Ms. Darbus, of course, held her detention on the stage of the school's theatre. The detainees' punishment was painting scenery, mopping the stage, and binding scripts.

Sharpay satisfied her requirements by telling Ryan how to paint a prop - and watching as he did it. Chad was trying to assemble a piece of scenery, but he was hopeless. All his agility and finesse on the basketball court translated to total clumsiness when he picked up a hammer. Troy and Gabriella were working on opposite sides of the stage, exchanging shy glances and trying to muster the courage to actually speak to each other.

Before either one of them could seize the moment, however, Taylor entered the auditorium and made a beeline for Gabriella. Taylor looked as if she had just won the lottery - and, considering that she was the Scholastic Club president, maybe she had.

She came to a halt in front of Gabriella and said, beaming, "The answer is yes!"

"Huh?" Gabriella was lost.

"Our Scholastic Decathlon team has its first competition next week, and there's certainly a chair open for you," Taylor said excitedly. She reached into her purse and pulled out a sheaf of newspaper articles about Gabriella's academic achievements.

Gabriella was stunned. "Where did those come from?"

"Didn't you slip them in my locker?" Now Taylor was confused.

"Of course not." Gabriella was more than confused - she was upset. She had wanted to pass for average, well, as close to average as she could. Now that plan was destroyed.

Sharpay stood to one side, pretending not to listen even as she listened as hard as she could.

Taylor quickly regrouped. "Well, we'd love to have you on the team. We meet almost every day after school." Then she had a quick flash of how much better their team would be if Gabriella joined, and added, “Please?”

“I need to catch up on the curriculum here before I think about joining any clubs . . .” Gabriella started hesitantly.

Sharpay whipped around. If there was any time to join this conversation, she thought, it was now. “But what a perfect way to get caught up, meeting with the smartest kids in the school. What a generous offer, Taylor!”

Gabriella looked from one girl to the other, feeling trapped. She was saved by Ms. Darbus, who walked onto the stage from the wings and said, “So many new faces in here today.” She stared at them meaningfully. “I hope it doesn’t become a habit, though the Drama Club can always use an extra hand. Now, as we work, let’s probe the mounting evils of cell phones. My first thought on the subject is – ”

Chad could recognize the beginning of a boring, long-winded lecture when he heard one. He quickly tried to hide inside a fake tree.

No luck. He could still hear Ms. Darbus, droning on. . . .

As Ms. Darbus listed all the problems with mobiles, the basketball team was taking the court for after-school practice. Coach Bolton entered and blew his whistle for practice to start.

"Okay, let's get rolling. Two weeks to the big - "

Then he paused and looked around. Something was wrong, he thought. Something was missing. Someone was missing. . . .

"Where are Troy and Chad?"

"Perhaps the most heinous example of cellphone abuse is ringing in the theatre," Ms. Darbus was saying. "What temerity! For the theatre is a temple of art, a precious cornucopia of creative energy . . ."

Only Ryan and Sharpay were still listening. They nodded soberly in agreement.

Chad was now asleep inside the fake tree. He was even snoring.

Just as everyone thought they might faint from boredom, Coach Bolton ran into the auditorium, the light of battle shining in his eyes.

"Where's my team, Darbus?!" he yelled. "And what the heck are they doing here!?"

Ms. Darbus pulled herself to her full height and said icily, "It's called crime and punishment . . . Coach Bolton." She swept her arm toward the stage and added, "And proximity to the arts is cleansing for the soul."

Unfortunately, Chad chose that moment to suddenly wake up and fall out of his fake tree.

Coach Bolton held his temper and said to Ms. Darbus, as quietly as he could, "May we have a word?" He pointed to Troy and Chad and snapped, "You two, into the gym. Right now."

Troy and Chad jumped up, overjoyed at their sudden release from prison. As they dashed for the door, Troy reached into the bucket and grabbed his mobile.

And then they were gone. Gabriella had watched them the whole way.

* * *

Principal Matsui sat behind his desk, looking with resignation at the school's basketball coach and drama teacher. The coach was angry. The drama teacher was defiant. And Principal Matsui was starting to get that familiar feeling of heartburn. . . .

"If they have to paint sets for detention, they can do it tonight, not during my practice," the coach said.

Ms. Darbus appealed to the principal's sense of fair play. "If these were theatre performers instead of athletes, would you seek special treatment?"

"Darbus, we are days away from the biggest game of the year," Coach Bolton said, exasperated.

"And we are in the midst of auditions for our winter musical, as well," the drama teacher shot back. "This school is about more than young men in baggy shorts flinging balls for touchdowns."

"Baskets," the coach said through gritted teeth. "They shoot baskets."

Principal Matsui sighed wearily. "Listen, guys, you've been having this argument since . . . let me think . . ." He raised his voice. ". . . *since the day you both started teaching here!*" In a more reasonable tone, he added, "We are one school, one student body, one faculty. Can we not agree on that?"

The coach and drama teacher stared at him in disbelief. Clearly, they weren't going to agree on anything.

The principal shook his head and picked up a minibasketball from his desk. He tossed it toward the small basketball hoop on his wall and asked, "How's the team looking, anyway? Troy got them whipped into shape?"

Ms. Darbus could only roll her eyes.

Having won his latest skirmish with Ms. Darbus, Coach Bolton returned to the gym. He paced in front of his team and reminded them of the sad truth they all knew. "The West High Knights have knocked us out of the playoffs three years running. Now we're one game away from taking the championship right back from them."

He stopped to look directly at each player in turn. "It's time to make our stand. The team is you, and you are the team. And the team doesn't exist unless each and every one of you is fully focused on our goal."

He focused on Troy and Chad, and added meaningfully, "Am I clear?"

They nodded, as the whole team erupted into their cheer. "Wildcats! Getcha head in the game!"

Coach Bolton nodded, satisfied. They were pumped up. They were ready. And they were going to win!

Ms. Darbus's detention was over, and Taylor and Gabriella were finally free. As they walked across the courtyard together, Taylor said, "We've never made it out of the first round of the Scholastic Decathlon. You could be our answered prayer."

Gabriella smiled. She was flattered, but she

didn't budge. "I'm going to focus on my studies this semester and help my mum get the new house organized. Maybe next year."

"But - " Taylor began.

Gabriella searched her mind for some way to change the subject, and immediately thought of a topic she was most curious about. "What do you know about Troy Bolton?"

"Troy?" Taylor raised her eyebrows in surprise. "I wouldn't consider myself an expert on that particular subspecies." Six cheerleaders were approaching them, walking in a pack, as usual. Taylor's eyes sparkled with mischief as she added, "However, unless you speak cheerleader, as in - " She put on an enthusiastic, cheerleader voice and said breathlessly, "'*Isn't Troy Bolton just the hottie superbomb?*'"

On cue, the cheerleaders nodded and squealed enthusiastically.

"See what I mean?" Taylor said to Gabriella.

Gabriella laughed. "I guess I wouldn't know how to speak cheerleader."

Taylor nodded, happy to have made her point. "Which is why we exist in an alternative universe to Troy-the-basketball-boy."

Gabriella nodded. She knew that Taylor was right. In every high school, there were the brainiacs, the jocks, the band kids, the cheerleaders, the slackers . . . And every group was its own clique. No one ever moved from one clique to another. No one.

Still . . .

"Have you tried to get to know him?" she asked.

Taylor just laughed. "Watch how it works in the cafeteria tomorrow when you have lunch with us. Unless you'd rather sit with the cheerleaders and discuss the importance of firm nail beds."

"My nail beds are history," Gabriella said, smiling as she held up her hands to illustrate her point.

Taylor laughed and held up her hands in turn. Her nails looked just as bad as Gabriella's.

"Sister!" she cried, and they slapped hands in brainiac solidarity.

It was almost dark, but Troy was still in his backyard, shooting hoops. His father watched approvingly; his boy had moves, he thought. Good moves. Great moves, in fact.

He had to make sure Troy didn't lose focus. Not now.

"I still don't understand this detention thing," he said.

"It was my mess-up," Troy answered quickly, hoping this wouldn't turn into a big discussion. "Sorry, Dad."

"Darbus will grab any opportunity to bust my chops, and yours, too," his father reminded him.

Troy nodded, but his mind was on other things. After a moment, he asked hesitantly, "Dad, did you ever think about trying something new but were afraid of what your friends might think?

"You mean working on going left?" his dad asked. "You're doing fine."

Troy sighed but tried again. "I meant - what if you try something really new and it's a disaster, and all your friends laugh at you?"

"Then maybe they're not your friends," his father said. "That was my whole point about 'team' today. You guys have to look out for each other. And you're their leader."

"Yeah, but - " Troy was getting frustrated. He was really confused here, what with Gabriella and the musical and the way he had felt singing with her, and all his dad could think about was the basketball game.

"There are going to be college scouts at our game next week, Troy," his father said, as if Troy needed reminding. "Do you know what a scholarship is worth these days?"

"A lot?" Troy said. He didn't need to ask. He knew that a basketball scholarship could pay for four years of college. It would really help his parents financially. And it would help set him up for the future.

His father nodded. "Focus, Troy."

And Troy nodded in agreement. That's what he had to do. Focus. Concentrate on basketball. Don't think about anything else - not even singing.

Especially not singing.

CHAPTER FIVE

The next morning, Troy entered his homeroom class. The first person he saw was Gabriella. He sneaked a peek at her and realized she was looking at him, too. They both smiled sheepishly and looked away as Ms. Darbus said sternly, "I expect we learned our homeroom manners yesterday, people, correct?"

Everyone nodded obediently.

"If not, we have dressing rooms that need painting," she warned. "Now, a few announcements. This morning during free period is your chance for musical auditions, both singles and pairs. I'll be in the theatre until noon, for those bold enough to explore the wingspan of their latent creative spirit."

Behind Troy, Chad rolled his eyes at this and leaned forward to whisper, "What time is she due back on the mother ship?"

His buddies snickered. Troy smiled uncomfortably. As he sat through the rest of homeroom, he tried to focus. Basketball, he kept saying to himself. Keep your eye on the prize, Troy. Don't think about anything except basketball.

When Ms. Darbus released the class, everyone piled out into the hallway. Chad quickly caught up with Troy. "Hey, Troy . . . the whole team's hitting the gym during free period. What are you going to have us run?"

Troy looked shifty. "Can't make it. I've got to catch up on homework."

Chad did a double take. "What?! Hello, this is only the second day back, dude," he protested.

"I'm not even behind yet, and I've been behind on homework since preschool."

Troy smiled and shrugged. "Catch you later," he said, then melted away in the crowd.

Chad looked after him, puzzled. "Homework?" he asked himself. "No way." He followed Troy, determined to figure out this mystery.

Chad would never make a good spy, Troy thought, catching a glimpse of his buddy out of the corner of his eye. He saw an open classroom door and quickly ducked inside. He saw Chad peer inside, and started talking to a couple of students as a cover. Then someone passing in the hall called out to Chad. As soon as Troy saw that his friend was distracted, he slipped out the back door of the classroom, scooted down the hall, and hurried down a stairwell.

The stairwell led outside to the courtyard. As Troy darted across the open area, he suddenly saw his father walking toward him. Thinking fast, Troy hid behind a wall, then opened the door to the automotive shop. He slipped inside just as his father approached.

Funny, Coach Bolton thought, *I could have sworn I just saw Troy. . . .* He looked around, but his son was nowhere in sight. The coach shrugged. *I must be seeing things. Must be the pressure of the big game,* he thought, and went on.

Troy's evasive skills and fast footwork came in handy as he moved quickly around the large pieces of equipment in the auto shop. As he reached the door, the auto-shop teacher approached.

". . . shortcut . . ." Troy explained quickly. ". . . late for class . . ." Then he ducked out the door, ran down the hall, and entered the school theatre from the backstage.

He peered out through the stage curtains and saw dozens of kids arriving, eager to try out. He spotted the caretaker's cart with a mop and bucket. He turned the mop upside down and used it as cover as he rolled the cart down a ramp, along the side of the theatre and into the shadows at the back of the auditorium.

From his safe hiding place, he watched as Ms. Darbus stepped onto the stage and began the auditions in her trademark dramatic style.

"This is where the true expression of the artist is realized, where inner truth is revealed through the actor's journey, where - " She stopped suddenly to glare around the theatre.

". . . WAS THAT A CELL PHONE?" she snapped.

Kelsi, the composer of this year's musical, was seated at a piano onstage. She answered Ms. Darbus timidly. "No, ma'am, it was the recess bell."

Ms. Darbus nodded, satisfied that her domain had not been invaded. "Those wishing to audition must understand that time is of the essence, we have many roles to cast, and the final callbacks will be next week. First, you'll sing a few bars, and then I will give you a sense of whether or not the theatre is your calling. Better to hear it from me than from your friends. Our composer, Kelsi Neilsen, will accompany you, and be available for rehearsals prior to callbacks. Shall we?"

She took a seat in the front row and braced herself for what was to come. She had too many years of experience with student auditions. She knew it wasn't going to be pretty.

The first student, a shy boy with a slightly flat voice, took the stage. Kelsi began playing the audition song, "What I've Been Looking For," and he sang along. When they'd finished, Ms. Darbus thought that it hadn't been *horrible*, but it certainly wasn't up to her high standards. Next came Susan, whose off-key voice and overly enthusiastic gestures were . . . well, Ms. Darbus thought, they were just scary bad. She winced as Susan belted out the song.

At the end of Susan's audition, Ms. Darbus put on a fake smile and said, "That's nice, Susan," adding, "perhaps best saved for a family gathering."

Then Alan bounded up, smiling. He was a very snappy dresser, but when he opened his mouth, Ms. Darbus realized sadly that he was a terrible singer.

She told him, "Alan, I admire your pluck. As to your voice . . . those are really nice shoes you're wearing. Next . . ."

Next was Cyndra, whose high-pitched wail made Ms. Darbus grimace. "Ah, Cyndra, what courage to pursue a note that's never been accessed in the natural world," she said, trying to be positive. "Bravo." She quickly corrected herself - after all, if there was one thing Ms. Darbus knew, it was theatre terminology. Bravo was said to congratulate a male singer, while brava was said to a female. "Brav*a*!" she said to Cyndra. "How about . . . the spring musical?

She thought she had reached her breaking point, but that was before she saw the next audition, a boy and a girl who made strange gestures and performed slow somersaults as they chanted the lyrics in a hypnotic monotone.

"Okay . . ." Ms. Darbus finally said. "That was . . . just plain disturbing. Go see a counsellor."

As Troy watched the auditions wistfully, he felt a tap on his shoulder. It was Gabriella.

"Hey! You decided to sign up for something?" she asked.

"No," he answered. "You?"

She shook her head. "No." Then she took in his "disguise." "Why are you hiding behind a mop?"

Embarrassed, he awkwardly pushed the mop out of the way.

Gabriella looked at him knowingly. "Your friends don't know you're here, right?"

He hesitated, then admitted the truth. "Right." He glanced at the stage, where the auditions - and Ms. Darbus's putdowns - were continuing. "Ms. Darbus is a little . . . harsh."

"The Wildcat superstar is . . . afraid?" she teased him.

"Not afraid . . . just . . ." He hesitated again, then let his guard down. ". . . scared."

Relieved, Gabriella said, "Me, too." She looked at Ms. Darbus, who was dismissing yet another hopeful singer. "Hugely."

As they nervously watched Ms. Darbus, the teacher checked her clipboard and announced,

"For the lead roles of Arnold and Minnie, we only have one couple signed up." She smiled warmly at her star students. "Nevertheless, Ryan and Sharpay, I think it might be useful for you to give us a sense of why we gather in this hallowed hall."

This was just the moment Sharpay and Ryan were waiting for! They made grand entrances from opposite sides of the stage, and bowed to the almost-empty auditorium as if it were a Broadway theatre filled with a cheering audience.

Sharpay glared at Kelsi, who jumped as she realized that she was expected to clap for them. Quickly regrouping, Kelsi asked shyly, "What key?" and prepared to play.

But Ryan lifted a boom box and said smugly, "We had our rehearsal pianist do an arrangement." He hit the PLAY button, and he and his sister began their routine.

Their voices were great, Kelsi admitted to herself, and their dancing! They must have had a professional choreographer! But they had changed her soulful ballad into a fast, upbeat number. She couldn't help but feel disappointed as they sang.

They finished with a professional flourish and beamed proudly. They were good, and they knew they were good.

After that audition, everyone else knew it, too. The few kids who were gathering their courage to audition at the last minute quietly slinked out of the theatre, totally intimidated.

"Don't be discouraged!" Ryan called after them. "The theatre club doesn't just need singers, it needs fans, too! Buy tickets!"

Kelsi gathered her courage and approached Sharpay and Ryan. "Actually, if you do the part . . . with that particular song, I was hoping you'd – "

"*If* we do the part?" Sharpay interrupted her. "Kelsi, my sawed-off Sondheim, I've been in seventeen school productions. And how many times have *your* compositions been selected?"

"This is the first time," Kelsi admitted.

"Which tells us what?" Sharpay demanded.

Kelsi paused, not sure what answer was expected of her. "That I should write you more solos?"

Sharpay shook her head. "It tells us that you do *not* offer direction, suggestion, or commentary," she said condescendingly. "And you should be thankful that Ryan and I are here to lift your music out of its current obscurity. Are we clear?"

"Yes, ma'am," Kelsi said, thoroughly cowed. Then she caught herself. "I mean, Sharpay."

"Nice talking to you," Sharpay said in a tone of dismissal. She and Ryan turned on their heels and left with the regal stride of future superstars.

Kelsi began gathering her music, her pulse racing after this close encounter with celebrity ego.

"Okay, we're out of time, so if we have any last-minute sign-ups?" Ms. Darbus announced. She looked around the room. "No? Good. Done."

She tossed her clipboard into her shoulder bag and began to leave. Gabriella took a deep breath. It was now or never, she thought. Before she could have second thoughts, she ran up to the drama teacher.

"I'd like to audition, Ms. Darbus."

Ms. Darbus shook her head. "Timeliness means something in the world of theatre, young lady. Plus, the individual auditions are long, long over. And there were simply no other pairs."

Then, out of the darkness, Troy's voice said, "I'll sing with her." He moved from the shadows to stand with Gabriella.

"Troy Bolton?" The drama teacher looked more than taken aback. She looked suspicious. "Where's your . . . sport posse, or whatever it's called?"

"Team," Troy said helpfully. "But I'm here alone. Actually," he smiled at Gabriella, "I'm here to sing with her."

"Yes, well, we treat these shows very seriously here at East High," Ms. Darbus sniffed.

"I called for the pairs audition, and you didn't

respond." She pointed to the clock. "Free period is over." Then, in an effort to sound gracious, she added, "Next musical, perhaps."

As she headed for the back of the auditorium, Kelsi started to leave the stage, clutching her sheet music. She was so distracted by all the drama - on and off the stage - that she tripped over the piano leg and sprawled to the floor. Her pages of music scattered everywhere.

Troy jumped up onstage, lifted her up, and began helping her collect the papers. Kelsi didn't lift a finger to help - she was too stunned. Troy Bolton, the Troy Bolton, the school's star basketball player, was helping her? She stared at him, frozen.

Troy didn't notice the effect he was having on Kelsi. "You composed the song that Ryan and Sharpay just sang?" he asked.

Speechless, Kelsi nodded.

"And the entire show?" he asked.

Again, Kelsi managed to nod. Barely.

"That's way cool," he said, truly impressed. "I

can't wait to hear the rest of the show." When she didn't answer, he went on. "Why are you so afraid of Ryan and Sharpay? It's your show."

Kelsi was so startled, she actually blurted out a couple of words. "It is?"

"Isn't the composer of a show like the playmaker in basketball?" he asked.

"Playmaker?" Kelsi hadn't ever heard that term, but she liked the sound of it.

"The person who makes everyone else look good," he explained. "Without you, there *is* no show. You're the playmaker here, Kelsi."

"I am?" Kelsi had never thought of it that way before. But now that Troy Bolton - *the* Troy Bolton! - had said it, she had to admit, it made a certain kind of sense. Feeling bold and strong for the first time, she sat at the piano and asked, "Do you want to hear the way that duet is supposed to sound?"

She began playing the audition song that Ryan and Sharpay had rearranged. She played it more slowly, with feeling and soul. Troy and Gabriella listened with growing appreciation.

"Wow, now that's really nice," Troy said.

Kelsi pushed the music toward Troy.

He looked at it. Did he dare?

Gabiella looked at it, too, feeling tempted.

Then Troy began to sing softly:

"It's hard to believe
That I couldn't see
You were always there beside me"

Gabriella soon joined in, a little more boldly.

"Thought I was alone
With no one to hold"

When they sang together, the harmonies melded perfectly.

They both felt the same glow they had felt on New Year's Eve. Kelsi beamed as she listened to this simple, pure interpretation of her song. It was the way she had dreamed it would sound.

As they finished, Ms. Darbus stepped forward from the darkness by the back door. She had been watching and listening the entire time. And what she had seen and heard had surprised her.

As she wrote their names on her clipboard, she called out, "Bolton, Montez, you have a call-back. Kelsi, give them the duet from the second act. Work on it with them."

The bell rang. Ms. Darbus strode off to her next class as Troy and Gabriella looked at each other, totally stunned. Now what?

Kelsi handed them the music and said eagerly, "If you want to rehearse, I'm usually in the music room during free period and after school . . . and sometimes even during biology class."

All was quiet until the next morning. Then, Sharpay walked into school. She checked out the sheet that Ms. Darbus had posted, listing who had to take part in a second round of auditions. And she saw the dreaded phrase. . . .

"CALLBACK!!!" Her scream echoed through the halls of East High.

Ryan rushed to her side and read aloud from the sheet. " 'Callback for roles of Arnold and Minnie, next Thursday, 3:30 P.M. Ryan and Sharpay Evans. Gabriella Montez and Troy Bolton.' "

"Is this some kind of joke?" Sharpay demanded angrily. "They didn't even audition."

"Maybe we're being punked?" Ryan suggested. "Maybe we're being filmed right now. Maybe we'll get to meet Ashton!"

"Shut up, Ryan!" Sharpay snarled.

By this time, a crowd of students had gathered. Troy's teammates Chad, Jason, and Zeke were among the students staring at the list.

Chad saw Troy's name. An expression of complete and utter horror crossed his face. "WHAT?!!!!!" he yelled.

By lunchtime, the news that Troy and Gabriella had tried out for the musical had spread throughout the school. As students entered the cafeteria, they took their usual seats. Jocks sat with jocks. Brainiacs sat with brainiacs. Drama kids sat with drama kids. Skater dudes, cheerleaders, punks . . . each sat with their own kind.

That was the way the world was meant to be. Orderly. Predictable. Understandable.

Sharpay held court at the head of the drama kids table. Kelsi sat at the far end, listening to every word, but keeping quiet, as usual.

"How dare she sign up," Sharpay said. "I've already picked out the colours for my dressing room."

"And she hasn't even asked our permission to join the Drama Club," Ryan pointed out supportively.

"Someone's got to tell her the rules," Sharpay decided.

"Exactly," her brother agreed. He thought for a moment, then asked, "What are the rules?"

As if he was just waiting for that cue, Zeke, a tall, burly basketball player with a killer smile, began singing. The other jocks gathered around, curious. Zeke looked at them, took a deep breath, and admitted, "If Troy admits he sings, then I can tell my secret." He whispered to them, "I bake."

"What?" Chad couldn't believe what he had heard.

But now that he had confessed, Zeke felt that he had been set free. "I love to bake," he said. "Scones, strudel, even apple pandowdy." He was too caught up in his enthusiasm to stop. "I dream of making the perfect crème brûlée," he said as Chad buried his face in his hands.

The jocks were horrified. Urgently, they sang:

"No, no, no, nooooooooooooo
Stick to the stuff you know
If you wanna be cool
Follow one simple rule
Don't mess with the flow, no no
Stick to the status quo"

Zeke had started something. Over at the brainiacs table, Martha Cox, a studious girl who wore glasses and a plain skirt and jumper, suddenly jumped up from the table, threw her arms wide and exclaimed, "Hip-hop is my passion! I love to pop, lock, break, and jam."

She demonstrated a few moves, and one of the brainiac boys got worried. "Is that legal?" he asked the table.

Martha turned to the worried boy and said, "It's just . . . dancing. And the truth is, sometimes I think it's even cooler than - " She took a deep breath, gathered her courage, and finished. " - homework!"

Her friends looked as if they were about to faint.

Meanwhile, across the cafeteria, a skateboarder stood up and confessed, "If Troy can be in a show, then I'm coming clean." He hesitated, then gave it up. "I play the cello."

"Awesome," said another skateboarder. "What is it?"

His friend mimed playing the cello, but saw only confusion in the other boarder's face.

"A saw?"

"No, it's like a giant violin," the first boarder explained.

"Do you have to wear a costume?" the second boarder asked.

"Tie and coat," the unmasked cello player said.

"That's uncalled for!" his friend exclaimed.

The spirit of rebellion was building, however! The skater dude jumped up on his table and enthusiastically mimed playing the cello. Brainiac Martha was busting out some cool hip-hop moves from the top of her table, dancing and swaying to the rhythm in her head.

The students who had confessed their secret loves were now all standing on their respective cafeteria tables as if they were on stages, singing their hearts out.

Finally, Sharpay had had enough! She shouted, "Everybody, quiet!" Her voice echoed through the room. All the students stopped and stared at Gabriella and Taylor, who had just entered the cafeteria and picked up their lunch trays.

Gabriella noticed the attention and said nervously, “Why are they pointing at you?”

“Not me,” Taylor replied. “You.”

“Because of the callback?” The memory of that horrible church choir experience flooded back into Gabriella’s mind. “I can’t have people stare at me. I really can’t.”

As Gabriella and Taylor wove through the crowd to a table, Gabriella stumbled. Her tray went flying and spilled chili fries, ketchup, and melted cheese all over . . . Sharpay.

Sharpay stood still, stone-faced, and Gabriella tried to clean the food from Sharpay’s blouse. It only made the mess worse.

At that moment, Troy entered the cafeteria and noticed what was going on. He headed over to help Gabriella, but Chad quickly intercepted him. “You can’t get in the middle of that, Troy,” his buddy warned. “Far too dangerous.”

He dragged Troy over to the safest place in the

room: their usual table. Troy looked around and realized that the cafeteria was buzzing with energy and excitement.

"What's up?" he asked.

"Oh, let's see," Chad answered. "You missed free-period workout yesterday to audition for some heinous musical. Suddenly people are . . . confessing. Zeke is baking . . . crème brûlée."

Troy frowned, trying to follow all this. This was a lot of confusing information, so he seized on the easiest point to clear up. Crème brûlée?

"What's that?"

"A creamy, custardlike filling with a caramelized surface," Zeke said, happy to finally be able to talk about his secret passion. "Very satisfying."

Chad rolled his eyes. This was getting out of control! "Shut up, Zeke!" he yelled. Then he turned to Troy. "Do you see what's happening? Our team is coming apart because of your singing thing. Even the drama geeks and brainiacs suddenly think they can . . . talk to us. The skater dudes are . . . mingling. People think they can suddenly . . . do other stuff! Stuff that's . . . *not their stuff!*"

He pointed dramatically to the kids sitting at Sharpay's table. "They've got you thinking about show tunes, when *we've* got a playoff game next week!"

At this moment, Ms. Darbus walked into the cafeteria and noted the unusual sense of turmoil among the students. She spotted Sharpay, who was trying, without success, to clean her blouse with a tissue.

"What happened here?" Ms. Darbus demanded.

"Look at this!" Sharpay cried indignantly. "That Gabriella girl dumped her lunch on me . . . on purpose! It's all part of their plan to ruin our musical."

She pointed an accusing finger at the jock table. "And Troy and his basketball robots are obviously behind it. Why do you think he auditioned?"

She sensed that she was convincing Ms.

Darbus that some sort of conspiracy was being hatched. She smiled a bit and went on smoothly, "After all the work you've put into this show, it just doesn't seem right."

Kelsi watched and listened as Sharpay worked on Ms. Darbus. But despite her new confidence, she still couldn't take on the queen of the Drama Club *and* Ms. Darbus.

At least, not yet.

Coach Bolton was eating a sandwich at his desk and reading the newspaper sports page, when Ms. Darbus suddenly barged in. He dropped the paper with a sigh - he had been having such a nice, peaceful lunch - as the drama teacher said, "All right, Bolton, cards on the table right now."

"Huh?" Sometimes Coach Bolton thought that all that make-believe was affecting Ms. Darbus's mind. She always seemed off in some other world, from what he could see.

"You're tweaked that I put your stars in detention, so now you're getting even?" Ms. Darbus was beside herself with rage.

"What are you talking about, Darbus?" The coach was honestly confused.

"Your 'all-star' son turned up for my audition," Ms. Darbus said. "I give every student an even chance, which is the long and honourable tradition of the theatre - something you wouldn't understand - but if he's planning some kind of practical joke in my chapel of the arts - "

The coach grasped the one truth he knew he could cling to amid this barrage of nonsense. "Troy doesn't even sing."

"Oh, you're wrong about that. But I won't allow my *Twinkle Town* musical made into a farce - "

He could help it. He almost laughed in her face, but managed to choke it back at the last second. "*Twinkle Town*?" he asked.

Apparently, his poker face wasn't as good as he thought. Ms. Darbus knew he was laughing, and immediately assumed that he had sent Troy to audition as some kind of practical joke.

"See!" she cried. "I knew it! I knew it!"

Back in the cafeteria, Taylor and Gabriella were still trying to recover from the chaos that had erupted.

"Is Sharpay really, really mad?" Gabriella asked. "I said I was sorry."

"No one has beaten out Sharpay for a musical since kindergarten," Taylor explained.

"I'm not trying to beat anyone out," Gabriella protested. "We weren't even auditioning. We were just . . . singing."

Taylor shook her head. "You won't convince Sharpay of that," she warned. "If that girl could figure out how to play both Romeo and Juliet, her own brother would be aced out of a job."

"I told you, it just . . . happened." Then she admitted the real truth. "But . . . I liked it. A lot."

She sighed and then asked Taylor the question she had been wondering about ever since New Year's Eve. "Do you ever feel like there's this whole other person inside of you, just looking for a way to come out?"

Taylor gave her a sharp look. "No," she said decisively.

The bell rang to signal the end of the lunch period. Sharpay stalked out of the cafeteria, but not before leveling a death-ray glance at Gabriella.

Then Zeke stepped up to stop Sharpay. He was fizzing with happiness, now that his secret love of baking was out in the open.

"Hey, Sharpay," he said. "Now that Troy's going to be in your show . . ."

"Troy Bolton is *not* in my show!" she snapped.

Zeke pushed on, undeterred. "I thought maybe you'd like to come to see me play ball some time. . . ."

Sharpay tossed her head and said grandly, "I'd rather stick pins in my eyes."

He frowned at her, puzzled. "Wouldn't that be awfully uncomfortable?"

She rolled her eyes in exasperation. "Evaporate, tall person!" she said as she stormed away.

Crestfallen, Zeke called after her, "I bake . . . if that helps."

The next day, Gabriella opened her locker and found a note. She read it quickly, then looked at a yellow door at the end of the hall. She was a little confused - and very intrigued.

She opened the door and found a staircase that led up to the roof. As she opened the door and stepped out into the beautiful, sunny day, she saw Troy sitting on a bench. He was surrounded by lush plants, all being grown as hydroponic experiments.

"So this is your private hideout?" she asked, smiling.

"Thanks to the Science Club," Troy said. "Which means my buddies don't even know about it."

Gabriella wondered about that. His teammates didn't seem to be his only buddies.

"Looks to me like everyone on campus wants to be your friend," she pointed out.

"Unless we lose."

He seemed a little down about that, she thought. The pressure must be intense, especially since . . .

"I'm sure it's tricky being the coach's son," she said.

Troy shrugged. "It makes me practise a little harder, I guess. I don't know what he'll say when he hears about the singing thing."

"You're worried?" She was surprised. Troy seemed so cool, so confident. Not the type to worry. Ever.

But Troy nodded. "My parents' friends are always saying, 'Your son is the basketball guy, you must be so proud.' Sometimes I don't want to be the basketball guy. I just want to be . . . a guy."

Gabriella smiled with understanding. He didn't want to be the basketball guy any more than she wanted to be genius girl. They were both so much more than that. . . .

"I saw how you treated Kelsi at the audition yesterday," she said softly. "Do your friends know *that* guy?"

He shook his head. "To them, I'm the play-maker dude."

"Then they don't know enough about you, Troy." Gabriella paused, then decided it was time to share a confession of her own. "At my other schools I was the freaky math girl. It's cool coming here and being . . . anyone I want to be. When I was singing with you, I just felt like . . . a girl."

"You even looked like one, too," he teased her.

She laughed, glad to have the seriousness of the moment lightened a bit. "Remember in kindergarten you'd meet a kid, know nothing about them, then ten seconds later were best friends, because you didn't have to be anything but yourself?"

"Yeah . . ." Troy's voice was wistful.

"Singing with you felt like that," Gabriella said sincerely.

"I never thought about singing, that's for sure," Troy said. "Until you."

"So you really want to do the callbacks?" she asked.

He thought about it for a moment as he looked at her. Really looked at her. Then he smiled. "Hey, just call me freaky callback boy."

She smiled, a glowing smile of pure happiness. "You're a cool guy, Troy. But not for the reasons your friends think." He looked down, a little embarrassed, and she moved on quickly. "Thanks for showing me your top secret hiding place. Like kindergarten."

Then the bell rang, breaking the mood and making Troy realize he was late. And that meant detention!

The next day, Kelsi sat alone at the piano, playing with passion and energy. No one else was in the room. Just Kelsi and her music. Exactly the way she liked it.

Troy sat in a stairwell, practising his audition song. He kind of liked the way his voice echoed.

At that moment, Ryan rounded a corner and slowed down to listen. He could have sworn he heard someone singing. . . .

Meanwhile, Gabriella had found her own private spot with great acoustics: the girls' bathroom. She stood in front of the mirror and sang.

Sharpay was heading for class when she thought she heard the faint sound of singing. She turned her head to spot where it was coming from . . . there! She opened the bathroom door and went in, looking everywhere for the source of the music.

She found . . . nothing.

I've been rehearsing too much, Sharpay thought as she left the bathroom. I'm starting to hear that music everywhere I go!

Gabriella stepped out of the hiding place she had quickly found for herself and smiled.

Later that day, in the school's rehearsal room, Kelsi played the piano for Gabriella and helped her with her phrasing.

Then it was Troy's turn. He worked as hard as he could, but singing was harder than he thought. Just when he was getting frustrated beyond belief, Kelsi would stop to encourage him.

Just like basketball, he thought. You've gotta keep practising.

And he started to sing again.

The other basketball players were in the gym, warming up for practice. Coach Bolton kept checking his watch. Where was Troy? He frowned. Something was going on with that boy. Something weird. Something different. And it was getting in the way of his championship dream.

Coach Bolton didn't like it. He didn't like it at all.

He would have liked it even less if he had known where Troy was.

In detention. Again.

The only bright side was that Gabriella was

there, too. They stole glances at each other as they painted scenery. Each one was smiling a secret smile. Each one was hearing the audition song in their heads.

Finally, detention was over. Troy raced into the gym - only to find that practice was over, too.

The players headed toward the locker room. Hoping to recover a bit from his absence, Troy said to his father, "I'm going to stay awhile, work on free throws."

Coach Bolton nodded coldly in agreement. "Since you were late for practice . . . again . . . I think your teammates deserve a little extra effort from you."

He gave Troy a hard look, then headed for his office.

Troy sighed. He started shooting baskets, sinking one after the other.

Then Gabriella poked her head around the door. He smiled in welcome and waved her in.

She entered cautiously, looking around with curiosity. "Wow, so this is your . . . real stage."

"I guess you could call it that," he said. "Or just a smelly gym."

He bounced the ball over to her. She grabbed it and took a shot. It went in, and Troy turned to her, surprised.

"Whoa . . . don't tell me you're good at hoops, too?"

"I once scored forty-one points in a league championship game," she said, straight-faced.

"No way," he said, impressed.

"Yeah," she laughed, "the same day I invented the space shuttle and microwave popcorn."

He laughed, stole the ball back from her, took a shot, and missed. She grabbed it on the rebound and said, "I've been rehearsing with Kelsi."

"I know," he said. "Me, too. And I was late for practice. So if I get kicked off the team, it'll be on your conscience."

Gabriella looked startled. "Hey, I - "

"Gabriella," Troy said, laughing. "Chill."

She gave him a stern look for the teasing just

as Coach Bolton came back to the gym.

"Miss, I'm sorry, this is a closed practice," the coach said, his voice booming in the empty gym.

"Dad, practice is over," Troy protested.

"Not until the last player leaves the gym," the coach said. "Team rules."

Gabriella sensed the tension between them and quickly said, "Oh, I'm sorry, sir."

"Dad, this is Gabriella Montez," Troy said.

Gabriella looked at the coach with interest. So this was Troy's father. . . .

The coach looked at her with disapproval. "Your detention buddy?" he said.

Okay. Gabriella knew when it was time to leave. "I'll see you later, Troy," she said. "Nice to meet you, Coach Bolton."

"You as well, Miss Montez," the coach said, as he gave her a stern look.

Troy faced his dad. "Detention was my fault, not hers."

"You haven't missed practice in three years," his father pointed out. "That girl turns up and you're late twice."

Troy felt anger flare up in his chest. "'That girl' is named Gabriella, and she's very nice," he said sharply.

"Helping you miss practice doesn't make her 'very nice,'" his dad said, just as sharply. "Not in my book. Or your team's."

"She's not a problem, Dad," Troy said, frustrated. Why was his father - why was his coach - making such a big deal about this? "She's just . . . a girl."

"But you're not just 'a guy,' Troy." His father - and his coach - was equally frustrated. "You're the team leader, so what you do affects not only this team, but the entire school. Without you completely focused, we won't win the game next week. And playoff games don't come along all the time . . . they're something special."

Without warning, a series of memories ran through Troy's mind: Singing with Gabriella. Laughing with Gabriella. Talking with Gabriella.

"A lot of things are special," he said.

"You're a playmaker, not a singer," his father reminded him.

Exasperated, Troy yelled, "Did you ever think maybe I could be both?" He turned abruptly and headed for the locker room.

His dad watched him go, worried. He hoped he had been able to get through to Troy, but he feared that he hadn't.

Inside the hall between the locker room and the gym, Chad, Jason, and Zeke huddled together. They had been listening, wide-eyed, to the confrontation between Troy and his father.

Now they looked at one another and shook their heads.

This was not good. This was not good at all.

CHAPTER SIX

The next day, Chad sat next to Troy at a study table in the library. Without even saying hello, he started right in with the question on his mind - not to mention the minds of everyone on the team.

"What spell has this elevated-IQ temptress-girl cast that suddenly makes you want to be in a musical?" he asked.

"I just . . . did it," Troy sighed. "Who cares?"

"Who cares?" Chad looked injured. "How about your most loyal best friend?"

The librarian glared at him. "Quiet in here, Mr. Danforth."

Chad pointed at Troy. "It's him, Miss Falstaff, not me." Chad turned back to Troy, his voice more urgent now. "You're a hoops dude, not a musical-singer person. Have you ever seen Michael Crawford on a cereal box?"

"Who is Michael Crawford?" Troy asked.

"Exactly my point," Chad said, vindicated. "He was the Phantom of the Opera on Broadway. My mum saw that musical twenty-seven times and put Michael Crawford's picture in our refrigerator. Not on it, *in* it. Play basketball, you end up on a cereal box. Sing in musicals, you end up inside my mum's refrigerator."

Troy frowned, trying to follow this logic. "Why did she put his picture in her refrigerator?"

"One of her crazy diet ideas," he said dismissively. "I do not attempt to understand the female mind, Troy. That's frightening territory."

He looked up to see the librarian heading in their direction. He leaned over and whispered,

"How can you expect the rest of us to be focused on the game if you're off somewhere in leotards singing in *Twinkle Town*?"

"No one said anything about leotards. . . ." Troy sounded a little worried.

Chad seized his advantage. "Maybe not yet, my friend, but just wait! We need you, Captain. Big-time."

Oops. The librarian was looming over them. "Mr. Danforth!"

Chad pointed to Troy again. "I tried to tell him, Miss Falstaff!" he said, the picture of innocence. To further the illusion, he turned to Troy and added, "I really tried!"

Then he crept away, followed by the librarian's accusing glare. Troy sat very still, thinking hard about what Chad had said.

Inside the chemistry lab, Taylor and the other members of the Scholastic Club were hard at work, when Chad, Jason, and Zeke entered.

Chad walked up to Taylor and said, "We need to talk."

The two groups were deep in conversation when Sharpay and Ryan passed the open door of the chemistry lab. They stopped to look and listen.

"Something isn't right," Sharpay said.

Ryan nodded. "They must be trying to figure out a way for Troy and Gabriella to actually beat us out. The jocks rule most of the school, but if they get Troy into the musical, then they've conquered the entire student body."

"And if those science girls get Gabriella hooked up with Troy Bolton, the Scholastic Club goes from drool to cool," Sharpay gasped. Her eyes narrowed. "Ryan, we need to save our show from people who don't know the difference between a Tony Award and Tony Hawk."

Back in the chemistry lab, Chad had finished making his pitch to Taylor and her team.

"You really think that's going to work?" Taylor

When they sang together, Troy and Gabriella forgot how nervous they were about performing in front of a crowd.

"This is the first time I've done something like this," said Gabriella.

When the clock struck midnight, Troy thought, 'People kiss each other on New Year's Eve. Should I -?'

"We have zero tolerance on cell phones during class," said Ms. Darbus. "Welcome to East High, Miss Montez."

When Gabriella saw Troy in the hallway, her eyes widened in disbelief.

"I won't be signing up for anything here for a while," Gabriella said. "I just want to get to know the school."

"Oh . . . were you going to sign up, too? My brother and I have starred in all of the school's productions," Sharpay informed Gabriella.

"Troy, the music in those shows isn't hip-hop or rock or anything essential to the culture," Chad said.

"Our Scholastic Decathlon team has its first competition next week and there's certainly a chair open for you," Taylor told Gabriella.

"This morning during free period is your chance for musical auditions," announced Ms. Darbus.

"Why are you so afraid of Ryan and Sharpay?" Troy asked Kelsi. "It's your show."

Sharpay and Ryan were a little too proud of their audition.

When Troy and Gabriella sang together at the audition, the harmonies melded perfectly.

"I never thought about singing, that's for sure," Troy said. "Until you."

“What spell has this elevated-IQ temptress-girl cast that suddenly makes you want to be in a musical?” Chad asked.

Gabriella’s confidence grew as she sang with Troy at their callback audition.

asked. The other members of the Scholastic Club looked equally dubious.

"It's the only way to save Troy and Gabriella from themselves," Chad said with certainty.

Taylor looked at her team for their input. After a brief pause, they all nodded. After all, they needed Gabriella as much as the basketball team needed Troy.

"We start tomorrow," Chad said, satisfied.

The next morning, as students poured into the school, Chad looked around secretively, as if on a spy mission. He spotted Taylor across the courtyard and gave a quick nod, in the best secret agent style.

She rolled her eyes at his theatrics and met him in a corner.

"My watch says seven forty-five, mountain standard time," he said in a hushed tone. "Are we synched?"

Taylor never wore a watch. She had an infallible inner clock. "Whatever."

"Then we are on go mode for lunch period?" Chad asked. "Exactly 12:05?"

She nodded and handed him a small laptop with a video lens attached. "Yes, Chad," she said. "We're a go. But we're not Charlie's Angels, okay?"

He grinned. "I can dream, can't I?"

And they were off.

At exactly 12:05, the lunch bell rang. Dozens of students headed to the cafeteria for lunch, but Troy headed for the locker room.

He arrived to find his whole team waiting for him. As he stepped in the room, Jason closed the door behind him and stood in front of it, blocking it with his body.

Chad stood in the centre of the room next to a table covered with trophies and photos. He picked up one of the photos and held it up for Troy to see.

"'Spider' Bill Natrine, class of '99," Chad said. "MVP, league championship game."

He pointed to a trophy from that game.

Zeke held up the next photo.

"Sam Netletter, class of '02," he said. "Known far and wide as 'Sammy Slamma-Jamma.' Captain, MVP, league championship team."

He pointed to that trophy as Jason picked up the next photo.

" 'Thunderclap' Hap Haddon, '95," Jason said and pointed to the relevant trophy. "Led the Wildcats to back-to-back city championships. A legend."

"Yes, legends, one and all," Chad said, underlining the theme. "And do you think any of these Wildcat legends *became* legends by getting involved in musical auditions, just days before the league championship *playoffs*?"

The team stared intently at Troy and chanted in unison, "Getcha head in the game!"

"These Wildcat legends became legends because they never took their eye off the prize," Chad said. He was on a roll.

The team chanted again. "Getcha head in the game!"

Chad turned to the team and asked, "Now, who was the first sophomore ever to make starting varsity?"

The team smiled as one. "Troy!" they yelled.

Chad nodded. "So who voted him our team captain for *this* year?"

"Us!" the team yelled.

"And who is going to get their sorry butts kicked in Friday's championship game if Troy is worried about an audition?" Chad asked.

"We are," the team said together, depressed.

"Hey, there are twelve of us on this team," Troy protested. "Not just me."

Chad raised one eyebrow. "Just twelve? I think you're forgetting a very important thirteenth member of this squad - " He pulled out another photo.

It was a black-and-white photo of a kid in a basketball uniform. From the style of the uniform - and the style of the hair - it was clear this photo was old school.

Troy took a good look. His jaw dropped.

"That's my dad . . ." he whispered.

Chad propped the photo against an old trophy. "Yes, Troy, Wildcat basketball champion, class of 1981. Champion . . . father - and now coach. A winning tradition like no other."

Troy looked around at his team. What was going on? He felt as if his team was trying to deprogram him or something!

Meanwhile, Gabriella and the rest of the Scholastic Club had gathered in the chemistry lab with brown-bag lunches. Taylor was pointing to a series of photos and sketches on the dry-erase board. They showed the process of evolution, Taylor style.

She lectured, "From lowly Neanderthal and Cro-Magnon, to early warriors, medieval knights . . . all leading to . . ." She unscrolled the pièce de résistance, a full-length photo of an NBA player's body, with Troy's head superimposed on it. ". . . lunkhead basketball man! Yes, our culture worshipped the aggressor throughout the ages, and we end up with spoiled, overpaid, bonehead athletes who contribute little to civilization other than slam dunks and touchdowns. That is the inevitable world of Troy Bolton."

Gabriella smiled, not knowing what was coming.

Taylor went to another wall, saying, "But the path of the mind, the path we are on . . . ours is the path that has brought the world *these* people – "

She pointed to photos as she called out each name. "Eleanor Roosevelt . . . Frida Kahlo . . . Sandra Day O'Connor . . . Madame Curie . . . Jane Goodall . . . Oprah Winfrey, and so many others who the world reveres."

Gabriella nodded. There was no doubt those were admirable people. "But . . . what has this . . . I've got Kelsi waiting for me to rehearse. . . ."

"Gabriella, Troy Bolton represents one side of evolution . . . lunkhead basketball man," Taylor explained patiently. "And our side, the side of education and accomplishment, is the future of civilization. That's the side where you belong."

In the locker room, Troy was doing his best to defend himself to his team. "If you guys don't know that I'll put one hundred and ten percent of my guts into that game, then you don't know *me*."

"Well, we just thought – " Chad began.

"I'll tell you what *I* thought," Troy said. "I thought you were my friends – win together, lose together . . . teammates."

Chad tried to explain their side of the story. "But suddenly the girl and the singing – " He was standing next to Taylor's laptop with the video-link camera.

Troy sighed, tired of discussing this and tired of defending himself. "I'm for the team, I've always been for the team. She's just someone I met. . . ."

Troy didn't know it, but the laptop camera was transmitting the live feed of everything he was saying to the chemistry lab . . .

. . . where Gabriella, Taylor, and the rest of the Scholastic Club watched what Troy was saying.

". . . The singing thing is nothing, probably just a way to keep my nerves down, it doesn't mean anything to me," Troy was saying. "You're my guys and this is our team . . . Gabriella's not important. I'll forget the audition, forget her, and we'll go get that championship. Everyone happy now?"

Taylor froze the image on the screen. "Behold," she said. "Lunkhead basketball man. So, Gabriella . . . we'd love to have you for the Scholastic Decathlon."

Gabriella stared at the screen, crushed by what Troy said. They had shared so much - surely it had meant *something* to him?

The other girls awkwardly shuffled towards the door. No one looked at Gabriella. On her way out, Taylor said, "Do you want to grab some lunch?"

Gabriella shook her head. She just wanted to be alone.

Taylor nodded and left.

Just then, Gabriella heard noise from the quad below. She went to the window and looked out in time to see an impromptu pep rally. The basketball team was swarming around Troy, trying to pump him up for the big game.

Gabriella felt so sad, so alone. And, just as she had been doing since New Year's Eve, she started to express herself in song:

"It's funny when you find yourself
Looking from the outside
I'm standing here
But all I want is to be over there
Why did I let myself believe
Miracles could happen
'Cause now I have to pretend
That I don't really care"

She left the chemistry lab. The halls of East High were filled with trophy cases, banners, and murals. All she wanted was to get away from Wildcat spirit, and it was impossible.

She finally got to her locker. As she began putting books into it, Troy came up to her. He was beaming, filled with energy and high spirits from the pep rally.

"Hey, how ya doin'?" he called.

She didn't look at him.

"Listen, there's something I need to talk to you about, okay?" he went on.

"And here it is," she interrupted him. "I know what it's like to carry the load with friends. I get it. You've got your boys, Troy. It's okay. So we're good."

"Good about what?" he asked, puzzled. "I need to talk to you about the final callbacks."

She tried to smile. It was better if she ended this now, rather than let him do it. She could act like it was all her own idea. At least, she thought, I'll still have my pride. . . .

"I don't want to do the callbacks, either," she said quickly. "Who were we kidding? You've got your team, and now I've got my team. I'll do the Scholastic Decathlon, you win your championship. It's where we belong." She smiled bravely. "Go, Wildcats."

Now Troy was the one who was bewildered and hurt. "But I don't – "

Gabriella didn't let him finish. "Me either," she said firmly.

She pulled the sheet music from her locker, handed it to him, and walked away.

"Gabriella!" Troy called.

She didn't respond. The bell rang, signalling the start of the next class.

Troy stared after her, stunned and hurt.

CHAPTER SEVEN

Over the next few days, Gabriella and Troy became more and more depressed. Gabriella thought Troy had dumped her. Troy thought Gabriella had dumped him. And, even though their friends tried to cheer them up, nothing worked.

One day, during PE class, Chad, Jason, Zeke, and some other students were goofing around on the outside basketball court. They were passing a ball in a circle, fast and slick, just like the

Harlem Globetrotters. Laughing, they waved at Troy, inviting him to join them.

But Troy ignored them and headed over to the track for a jog instead, moving steadily away from his friends.

That evening, Troy shot baskets alone in his backyard. He missed a few baskets and slammed the ball down in frustration. His father watched from an upstairs window, worried. He knew something was wrong. He also knew it wasn't the right time to try to find out what it was.

At the Montez house, Gabriella was sitting by her bedroom window. She was surrounded by her books, but she wasn't reading. Instead, she was gazing out the window at the stars and trying not to cry.

Her mother opened the door, holding a portable phone. She held it out to Gabriella, indicating that the call was for her.

Gabriella just shook her head.

The next day, Gabriella and Troy happened to pass each other in the cafeteria. They glanced at each other, then away . . . then defused the awkward moment by moving on without saying a word.

Chad and Taylor saw the exchange from opposite ends of the room. They looked at each other and nodded. They'd seen enough. They could see the effect of what they'd done, and they knew that they'd screwed up, big-time.

Now they had to try to fix it. . . .

Troy was sitting by himself in the rooftop garden, glumly eating a sandwich. The door opened and Chad, Zeke, and Jason appeared.

"We just had another team meeting, Troy," Chad said.

"Wonderful," Troy answered. He tried to keep the bitterness out of his voice.

Chad swallowed hard. "We had a meeting

about how we haven't been acting like a team. Us, not you. The singing thing - "

"I don't want to talk about it," Troy said shortly.

"We just want you to know that we're going to be there cheering for you," Chad finished.

Troy looked up, surprised. "Huh?"

Zeke nodded furiously. "Yeah, Cap, if singing is something you want to do, we should be boosting you up, not tearing you down."

"Win or lose, we're teammates," Chad added. "That's what we're about. Even if you turn out to be the worst singer in the world - "

" - which we don't know, because we haven't actually heard you sing," Jason pointed out.

Troy sighed. It was great to finally have the support of his buddies, but it didn't mean anything anymore. "And you're not gonna hear me sing, dudes, because Gabriella won't even to talk to me, and I don't know why."

Chad and the boys exchanged uneasy glances. "We do," Chad finally said.

Zeke pulled a bag of cookies from his backpack and offered them to Troy. "Baked these fresh today. Want to try one before we tell you the rest?"

Inside the chemistry lab, Gabriella was surrounded by Taylor and the Scholastic Club.

"We're worse than jerks," Taylor was saying earnestly, "because we're mean jerks. We thought Troy Bolton and the singing thing was killing our chances to have you on our Scholastic Decathlon team."

"Why talk about it?" Gabriella said curtly. "I heard what he had to say. I'm on your team now. Done."

"No," Taylor sighed. "Not done." She hesitated, then admitted, "Chad knew he could get Troy to say things that would make you want to forget about the callbacks. We planned it. And we're embarrassed and sorry."

Gabriella absorbed the shock of that, but she said, "No one forced Troy to say anything." She took a deep breath and went on bravely. "And you know what? It's okay. We should be preparing for the decathlon now. So it's time to move on."

Taylor shook her head. She couldn't let this defeatist attitude go unchallenged. "No, it's not," she said in ringing tones. "The Scholastic Decathlon is . . . whatever. How you feel about us, and Troy, that's something else."

That evening, Mrs. Montez opened the front door to find Troy Bolton standing on her doorstep.

"Mrs. Montez, I'm Troy Bolton," he said politely.

Her eyes widened a little. So this was the Troy she had heard about from Gabriella! She smiled. "Oh . . . Troy . . ."

She glanced over her shoulder. Gabriella was standing on the stairs, just out of Troy's line of sight. She shook her head adamantly.

Mrs. Montez raised one eyebrow, but she got

the message. She turned back to Troy and said, "Well, Gabriella is a little busy with homework and such, so now's not really a good time. . . ."

"I made a mistake, Mrs. Montez, and I need to let Gabriella know that," he said in a rush. "Could you tell her that I came by to see her?"

She nodded and smiled as she closed the door. Troy Bolton, she thought. He certainly seems like a nice boy. . . .

As Troy left, he crossed the lawn and glanced up. He saw a light go on at the far end of the second story. There was a small balcony outside the window. Suddenly inspired, Troy took out his mobile and dialled Gabriella's number.

In her room, Gabriella saw Troy's photo come up on her mobile screen. After a long moment, she answered.

As soon as he heard her voice, Troy said in a rush, "What you heard the other day . . . none of that is true. I was sick of my friends riding me about singing with you, and I said things I knew would shut them up. I didn't mean any of it."

"You sounded pretty convincing to me," she said coolly.

Troy looked up. He could see Gabriella walking around in her room. He looked up at the balcony for a moment, then he looked at a nearby tree. Then he started climbing.

As he climbed, he continued to talk into the phone. "The guy you met on vacation is way more me than the guy who said those stupid things."

"Troy, the whole singing thing is making the school whack," Gabriella sighed. "You said it yourself, everyone is treating you different because of it."

Troy grabbed a branch and pulled himself a few feet higher. "Maybe that's because I don't want only to be the basketball guy anymore," he argued. "They can't handle it. That's not my problem, it's theirs."

He pulled himself up onto the balcony. Gabriella was only a few feet away, but her back was to him. She didn't know he was there.

She said, "But your dad – "

"This isn't about my dad," he said, still talking into the phone. "This is about how I feel. And I'm not letting the team down. . . . They let me down. I'm going to sing. What about you?"

"I don't know, Troy."

"You need to say yes," he said. "Because I brought something for you."

Gabriella looked confused. "What do you mean?"

Troy lowered his phone and began to sing to her, directly, sweetly, honestly.

"Start of something new
It feels so right
To be here with you . . . oh
And now . . . lookin' in your eyes
I feel in my heart
The start of something new"

Gabriella turned around to see Troy standing on the balcony outside her room.

"It's a *pairs* audition," he reminded her. Then he handed her the sheet music she had given back to him. After a long shared look, Gabriella began to smile.

The next few days were a whirlwind of activity for both of them. Troy led basketball practices with energy and authority, back on top of his game. Gabriella ran through formulas with the Scholastic Club, more focused and impressive than they had ever seen her. Then they would run out of their separate practices, meet in the hall, and dash for the rehearsal room to rehearse with Kelsi.

One day, Sharpay and Ryan came out of their own rehearsal and heard Gabriella and Troy singing.

"Wow, they sound good," Ryan said.

Sharpay turned on him. "We have to do something. Our callback is on Thursday, the basketball game and Scholastic Decathlon are on Friday." She stopped. An idea - a good idea, possibly a great idea - was forming. "Too bad all of these events aren't happening on the same day at the same time."

"Well, that wouldn't work," Ryan said with his usual naïveté, "because then Troy and Gabriella couldn't make the callback."

Sharpay gave him a look and waited for the implications to sink into her brother's dim brain.

Finally, his face lit up and he said, "I'm proud to call you my sister."

Later, Sharpay and Ryan cornered Ms. Darbus and spent some minutes talking earnestly to her.

Finally, Ms. Darbus said, "So if you're telling me, as copresidents of the Drama Club, that changing the callbacks is what's best for our theatre program . . . I might actually agree with you."

She walked away. Ryan scratched his head.

"Was that a yes?" he asked his sister.

She gave him a wink that said, "Mission accomplished."

What they didn't notice - because they never noticed Kelsi - was that the shy young composer was standing nearby and had witnessed the entire thing.

Including the wink.

The next morning, Troy and Gabriella got to school early so they could meet Kelsi and work in a little more rehearsal. They found her standing in front of the bulletin board, her face ashen.

The sign on the board said: MUSICAL AUDITIONS RESCHEDULED TO FRIDAY 3:30 P.M.

Troy and Gabriella stared glumly at those fatal words.

"Same time as the game - " Troy said.

"And the Scholastic Decathlon - " Gabriella added.

Chad and Taylor - accompanied, as always, by the basketball team and the Scholastic Club - gathered behind Troy and Gabriella.

"Well, I just don't know why they would do that," Taylor said, honestly puzzled.

"I smell a rat named Darbus," Chad said darkly.

"Actually, I think it's two rats, neither of them named Darbus," Kelsi said.

Everyone turned to see who had spoken. It took a minute - the petite Kelsi was almost lost among all the basketball players who towered over her.

"Do you know something about this, small person?" Chad asked.

Kelsi nodded. "Ms. Darbus might think she's protecting the show, but Ryan and Sharpay are pretty much only concerned with protecting themselves."

Chad's face tightened with anger. "Do you know what I'm going to do to those two over-moussed show dogs - "

"Nothing," Troy said quickly, taking command. "We're not going to do anything to them." He grinned. "Except sing, maybe."

Troy looked at each member of the basketball team and Scholastic Club. "This is only going to happen if we all work together," he said. "Who's in?"

The teams eyeballed each other. Then Chad held up a hand. Taylor high-fived it. Everyone broke out into grins.

They were in.

On the day of the callback auditions, basketball championship game, and Scholastic Decathlon showdown, emotions were running high.

To demonstrate their newfound sense of solidarity, Chad and the basketball boys presented Taylor with a cake that Zeke had baked. The icing read: "Scholastic Decathlon Today - Support Brain Fame!"

In return, Taylor and her girls handed Chad a banner that read: "Go Wildcat Hoopsters!"

Ms. Darbus watched them sardonically. How lovely, she thought. The basketball boys and the brainiac girls are making nice. . . .

Then Chad and the boys walked up to Sharpay and Ryan and zipped open their jackets. Each one had a letter on his T-shirt, spelling out the message: "Go, Drama Club!"

Chad gave Sharpay a huge smile.

Ms. Darbus looked around at the banner, the cake, the boys with letter T-shirts, and smiled in spite of herself.

"Well, it seems we Wildcats are in for an interesting afternoon," she said drily. But her eyes were twinkling.

CHAPTER EIGHT

At three o'clock, the halls of East High were empty. Quiet filled the school. There was a sense of anticipation –

– and then the bell rang!

Doors burst open and students rushed into the halls. The school was buzzing with excitement!

In the gym, the stands were full of spectators, cheering and clapping. The school band was playing, the cheerleaders were dancing up a storm, banners were waving in the air. . . . It was time to decide who were the champions, once and for all!

In the locker room, Troy sat alone on a bench. The rest of the team had run onto the court. He could hear the crowd being whipped into a frenzy.

All those hours of practice, all those drills, all that training . . . it all came down to this night.

His dad came into the room. "How're you feeling?"

"Nervous." Troy had to be honest.

"Me, too." His dad smiled. "Wish I could suit up and play alongside you today."

Troy grinned slightly. "Hey, you had your turn."

His father looked at him seriously. "Do you know what I want from you today?"

Troy nodded. His dad didn't have to tell him. "A championship."

His dad looked Troy straight in the eyes. "That'll happen or it won't," he said gently.

"What *I* want is for you to have fun. I know about all the pressure, and probably too much of it has come from me. All I really want is to watch my son having the time of his life, playing a game we both love. Give me that, and I'll sleep with a smile tonight, no matter how the score comes out."

Troy looked at his father. A strange feeling of relief spread through him. "Thanks, coa - " He corrected himself. " - Dad."

His father smiled at him and walked away.

Blackboards had been set up on each side of the choir room - the first round of the Scholastic Decathlon was about to begin. The walls were lined with tables where contestants could conduct experiments. A few dozen chairs had been set out for judges and spectators.

As the clock ticked down, each team gathered for a final briefing.

In the theatre, Kelsi played random tunes on the piano as a few spectators wandered into the large auditorium. Ryan and Sharpay did bizarre actor-prep exercises backstage: opening their mouths wide, uttering weird vocalizations, and falling back into each other's arms to demonstrate their absolute trust in each other.

In the choir room, the decathlon teams, all wearing lab coats, faced off for the opening bell.

Gabriella stood at a blackboard, poised to begin. The moderator signalled "go," and she and the star of the competing team began scribbling formulas as fast as they could.

In the theatre, Ms. Darbus was making yet another speech. "Casting the leads of a show is both a challenge and a responsibility, a joy and a burden," she said. "I commend you, and all young artists who hold out for the moon, the sun, and the stars – "

The five kids sitting in the auditorium just stared at her. They didn't have a clue about what she meant.

Ms. Darbus sighed, and tried to end on a grand note. "So . . . shall we soar together?" She checked her clipboard, just for form's sake, and called out, "Ryan and Sharpay?"

The brother-and-sister team made a grand entrance as their recorded music started. From the very first note, it was clear that this was a two-person musical, with light cues and choreography and moves that would put most Broadway dancers to shame.

As they started singing the chorus, Sharpay and Ryan moved into all-out choreography, with kicks, spins, turns, and leaps.

Meanwhile, in the gym, the two teams who would be battling for the championship finally faced each other in centre court. This was it - all the training, all the practice drills, all the pep talks led up to this . . . very . . . moment. . . .

The ref threw the ball for the opening tip-off, and the game began! From the very first seconds, the crowd was going crazy.

Even in the choir room, the Scholastic Decathlon team could hear the crowd noise. Everyone except Gabriella, that is. She was standing at the board, totally focused on what she had to do. As the timer ticked down, she and her opponent wrote formulas as quickly as possible.

Just one last number and - she finished seconds ahead of her opponent and slammed the timer button, stopping the clock.

The moderator quickly checked her answer, then nodded. Points to the Wildcat Scholastic team! As everyone cheered Gabriella, whose face was flushed with victory, Taylor peeked at the clock. It was 3:35 P.M.

She quietly moved over to her laptop and punched in a code, murmuring to herself, "All right, Wildcats, time for an orderly exit from the gym. . . ."

Immediately, the words "message transmitted" appeared on the screen. In the gym's utility room, a small wireless router had been patched into the electronic grid. Within seconds, the router started blinking . . . the mission had begun!

Suddenly, the electronic scoreboard blinked and random numbers began appearing where the score had been. The message board began flashing. The gym lights pulsed on and off.

The players stopped in midgame, baffled as to what was going on.

Principal Matsui didn't know what was happening either, but he did know school policy. He quickly took the microphone and said, "Well, we seem to have a little electronic gremlin here. I'm sure we'll figure this out. In the meantime, per safety regulations, we all need to make an orderly exit from the gym – "

As the gym slowly emptied, Chad grinned a private grin. Phase one of the mission had been executed!

Back in the choir room, Taylor quickly hit another key on her laptop. A beaker of blue liquid was sitting on a nearby hot plate, waiting for the experiment section of the competition.

Taylor's click turned on the hot plate, which heated the liquid, which began to gurgle, which created pressure that popped off the top of the beaker - which released an awesomely bad smell in the room.

Taylor smiled in quiet satisfaction as she saw first the moderator, then the spectators, begin to react to the smell.

Within seconds, everyone had rushed out of the room.

Taylor nodded. Phase two had just been completed.

In the theatre, Sharpay and Ryan were blissfully unaware of the other dramas that were taking place in the school. They ended their song with just as much energy as when they had started. They knew they had done phenomenally well, and they took extravagant bows.

"Do you see why we love the theatre, people?" Ms. Darbus said, almost overcome with pride and joy in her star pupils. "Well done."

She made a quick check of her list and then asked, in an offhand voice, "Troy Bolton and

Gabriella Montez?" She looked around. "Troy . . . Gabriella?"

But there was no sign of them.

Kelsi looked around nervously. "They'll be here!"

Ms. Darbus shook her head with little regret. "The theatre, as I've often pointed out, waits for no one. I'm sorry."

Kelsi gave one more despairing glance at the door, but there was still no sign of her friends. She sank back onto the piano bench, crushed.

"Okay, we're done here," Ms. Darbus said briskly, drawing a line through Troy and Gabriella's names. "Congratulations to all. The cast will be posted."

Slowly, Kelsi picked up her music folder and left the stage, totally dejected.

Then Troy and Gabriella came dashing in from opposite sides of the theatre.

"Ms. Darbus! We're here!" Troy yelled.

"I called your names," Ms. Darbus said sternly. "Twice."

"Please." Gabriella couldn't believe it. After all their work, all their planning . . .

The drama teacher was firm. "Rules are rules."

But as she turned to go, she saw that something different, unexpected, in fact, altogether astounding was happening! The theatre was starting to fill with people: students and spectators from the basketball game and Scholastic Decathlon; all the members of the basketball team, led by Chad; all the members of the Scholastic Club, led by Taylor . . . they were all coming to watch the auditions!

Sharpay and Ryan watched the gathering crowd, confused. This wasn't part of their plan! Still, the theatre is all about dealing with the unexpected, so Sharpay quickly said, "We'll be happy to do our number again for our fellow students, Ms. Darbus."

The teacher shook her head, still watching with amazement as the theatre filled to capacity. "I don't know what's going on here. But, in any event, it's far too late, and we don't have a pianist."

Ryan and Sharpay smiled, relieved. Ryan looked at Troy and shrugged. "Oh, well, that's showbiz," he said happily.

Desperate, Troy said, "We'll sing without music."

Then they heard a voice - previously a timid voice, now a surprisingly bold one - call out, "Oh, no, you won't!" Kelsi charged onto the stage. "Pianist here, Ms. Darbus!"

Sharpay gave her a warning glance. "You really don't want to do that."

Kelsi set her jaw. She had had enough of taking orders from egotistical drama queens. "Oh, yes, I really do!"

She opened the piano lid with a flourish, slapped down her music, and took a seat. "Ready onstage!"

Ms. Darbus's eyes widened with delight. "Now . . . *that's* showbiz!"

Troy and Gabriella picked up their microphones and turned to face the auditorium. It was packed with people, all waiting to hear them sing.

As Gabriella looked out at all those eager

faces, she felt her face turn red. Then her knees got weak, and her stomach flipped over, and she thought she might faint.

Their first audition had been for Ms. Darbus, and they hadn't even known she was listening! Now she had to face this huge crowd.

Kelsi hit a piano key, waiting for Troy and Gabriella's nod that they were ready to begin. No one nodded. Gabriella was standing absolutely still, as if she were frozen.

Kelsi started to play, hoping that the music would help relax Gabriella and that she would start singing.

But Gabriella couldn't even open her mouth. Kelsi stopped playing and looked at Troy. What should I do?

He nodded to her to start again. And then he began to sing, directly to Gabriella.

"We're soarin', flyin'
There's not a star in heaven that we can't reach
If we're tryin', yeah, we're breaking free"

When it was Gabriella's turn, she covered her mic and said, "I can't do it, Troy. Not with all these people staring at me."

Troy glanced at the crowd. People were starting to look confused. They were murmuring to each other, "What's wrong? Is she all right?"

He turned back to Gabriella and whispered, "Look at me. Right at me. Like the first time we sang together, like kindergarten, remember?"

She did. And when she looked into Troy's eyes, he looked back the same way he did at the karaoke contest. The spark of magic flared up again, but brighter and stronger. Gabriella could feel herself relax. She could feel herself smile. . . .

Troy made a signal to Kelsi, and she started playing again. Troy sang, heartfelt:

"You know the world can see us
In a way that's different
Than who we are"

Gabriella smiled even wider and sang the next two lines:

"Creating space between us
'Til we're separate hearts"

Then they sang together, in perfect harmony:

"But your faith
It gives me strength, strength to believe . . ."

As they continued, their confidence - and their trust in each other - grew. They began to sing as though they were the only ones in the room.

Everyone in the auditorium was transfixed by the powerful, real emotion that Troy and Gabriella were expressing through the song.

Coach Bolton wandered into the auditorium, wondering impatiently when the electronic malfunction would be fixed and the game could resume. He looked at the stage - and he couldn't believe what he was seeing! His son was singing, in public, and - he was really, really good!

Throughout the theatre, the music was casting its spell. The brainiac girls glanced at the basketball boys, and the two groups exchanged friendly smiles. The skater dudes nodded to the drama kids - hey, if this is musical theatre, it's cool, man. All the different groups, usually so separate, were united as they watched a completely unlikely pair - Troy dressed in basketball warm-ups and Gabriella wearing a lab coat - sing to each other with genuine emotion.

As the song ended, Troy and Gabriella gazed into each other's eyes. For one long moment, there was total silence. Then Kelsi stood up and began applauding. So did Coach Bolton. Ms. Darbus called out "Bravo!" and "Brava!" over and over again. And then the entire crowd was on their feet, roaring their approval.

Even Ryan and Sharpay started applauding - then they caught themselves and quickly stopped.

Before the applause ended, Troy and Gabriella gave each other a quick hug and rushed off. After all, they had some unfinished business to attend to. . . .

CHAPTER NINE

It was the last few seconds of the championship game. The Wildcats were behind. The clock was ticking down. . . .

Then Troy suddenly flew across the court, weaving between opponents, heading for the goal. Just as he had practised, he faked right, went left, threw the ball, and . . . NOTHING BUT NET! The buzzer sounded and it was a one-point Wildcat victory!

In the melee that followed, Coach Bolton

found his son and gave him a huge hug.

Ms. Darbus fought her way through the crowd. As she approached the coach, the old adversaries eyed each other for a moment . . . then they grinned and gave each other a high five.

As Gabriella got close to Troy, he called out, "What about your team?"

"We won, too," she said, excited and happy. They hugged each other in congratulations, just as Chad handed a basketball to Troy.

"Team voted you the game ball, Captain," he said. They high-fived each other, then he turned to Taylor. "So . . . you're going with me to the after-party, right?"

"Like on a date?" Taylor asked, shocked.

"Must be your lucky day." Chad grinned.

She laughed, and nodded. A week ago, she would have disagreed, but now . . . maybe Chad was right. Maybe it *was* her lucky day.

As Gabriella walked out of the gym, still beaming, Sharpay came up to her. "Well, congratulations," Sharpay said. "I guess I'm going to be the understudy in case you can't make one of the shows, so . . . break a leg."

Gabriella looked at her, startled.

Sharpay smiled - a real smile this time - and explained, "In theatre, that means good luck."

And now Gabriella smiled a real smile, too.

As she moved on, Zeke saw his chance and moved in on Sharpay.

"Sorry you didn't get the lead, Sharpay," he said. "But you're still really, really good. I admire you so much."

"And why wouldn't you?" asked Sharpay, who hadn't changed into a completely different person, after all. "Now bye-bye."

He shyly held out a bag of cookies. "I baked these for you. . . ." She took them as if they were her due, and he walked away.

Troy found Kelsi in the crowd and handed her the basketball. "Composer, here's our game ball. You deserve it . . . playmaker."

Kelsi nearly fainted. *She* was being handed the game ball by *Troy Bolton*! She got dizzy, just thinking about how much her life had changed in one short week. Dizzy and very, very happy. She broke into a huge grin and threw the ball in the air. . . .

And when it came down, East High School was a different place. It was a place where punk kids could talk to brainiacs, and jocks could hang out with drama kids. It was a place where everybody could follow the beat of their own drummer, and other people would cheer them on. In other words, it was a place where people could have fun . . . together.

After the huge celebration ended, people were still milling around, laughing, talking, and getting to know people they had never even noticed before.

That's when Sharpay came flying into the crowd, pushing people out of the way to get to Zeke.

"Your cookies are genius!" she yelled. "The

best things I've ever tasted. Will you make some more for me, Zeke?"

Zeke grinned. *Of course* he would bake for her! In fact . . . he waggled his eyebrows and said slyly, "I might even make you a crème brûlée."